TO SEIZE THE RAINBOW

Molly had been vastly indignant when
Christopher Ashburton, a total stranger,
had dared to kiss her. Now Molly knew
that Christopher was Lord Ashburton, a
wealthy Englishman practically engaged
to Lydia Frazier, the beautiful model—
and the governor's daughter. Had Molly
come so far only to find herself drawn to a
man who could never be hers? Suddenly
she was adrift on the beautiful turquoise
seas of New Zealand, hopelessly caught in
the shifting tides of love.

TO SEIZE THE RAINBOW

Jo Calloway

CHIVERS LARGE PRINT
BATH

Library of Congress Cataloging-in-Publication Data

Calloway, Jo.
  To seize the rainbow / Jo Calloway.
  ISBN 0–7927–1490–3 (lg. print)
  ISBN 0–7927–1489–X (lg. print: pbk.)
  1. Large type books. I. Title. II. Series.
[PS3553.A4244T6   1993]   92–30419
813'.54—dc20   CIP

British Library Cataloguing in Publication Data available

This Large Print edition is published by Chivers Press, England, and by Curley Large Print, an imprint of Chivers North America, 1993.

Published by arrangement with Donald MacCampbell, Inc.

U.K. Hardcover ISBN 0 7451 1815 1
U.K. Softcover   ISBN 0 7451 1826 7
U.S. Hardcover ISBN 0 7927 1490 3
U.S. Softcover   ISBN 0 7927 1489 X

Printed in Great Britain

TO SEIZE THE RAINBOW

CHAPTER ONE

Molly Rayner pressed close to the oval window of the jet plane. As the sun blazed down on the turquoise-green sea, she looked down at the tiny yachts dotting the ocean. Her feet, her hands, every nerve in her body, quivered. Perhaps it had been a reckless thing to do, but at least she had finally decided to do something. No more shivering along the city pavements in a heavy winter coat and fur-lined boots. Right or wrong, she had traded the cold winter in Pennsylvania for the summer warmth of New Zealand.

She had almost not come. When she read the first letter from the aunt she had never seen, the aunt she hardly knew existed, she discarded the request as a foolish notion. The very idea: to fly halfway around the world to help with a business she knew nothing about and to live with a woman she knew even less about, a woman who had left Pennsylvania forty years ago to marry a New Zealander. But a month later the second letter brought a different response. Many things had happened in the interim, among them, her breakup with Mitchell Holt, the man she had considered marrying. Reading the letter this time, she decided to go. Anything to rid herself of the loneliness she had never before experienced. It seemed she was destined to remain single. She roused herself from her thoughts as the captain's announcement echoed in the cabin.

'Ladies and gentlemen, in approximately five minutes we will be landing in Auckland, largest city of the North Island. The temperature is a warm seventy-nine, the sky clear. Speaking for myself and the crew, we wish you a pleasant visit in New Zealand. It has been our pleasure to serve you.'

Her eyes strayed about the long coach section of the plane. The stewardesses were smiling and talking briefly with wide-eyed, eager passengers. A moment later they returned to the rear of the plane and buckled themselves in their seats in preparation for landing.

Molly Rayner's jittery sensation heightened. Lifting her compact mirror to eye level, she studied herself momentarily. Would Aunt Cora be expecting a twenty-five-year-old, petite, dreamy-eyed girl, somewhat refined, but terribly shielded from life? Carefully smoothing a lock of fallen hair, she sighed. Would Cora Newcomb be disappointed in her? If this should be the case, what would she do on an island thousands of miles from home, halfway between the Equator and the South

Pole? She held her breath as the wheels touched the runway. She had one last frantic thought—Let this be the right decision!—before the jet swung into the unloading slot.

When the plane stopped, Molly stood, straightened her skirt, smoothed her hair, then stepped into the aisle and made her way from the plane.

Entering the modern terminal, she glanced at her watch. It was ten minutes to five. Her flight had arrived forty minutes late. Looking about the room hurriedly, she saw no sign of an elderly lady. A powerfully built, dark-haired man stood close to the ticket window, his head erect as he glared at the passengers. Not particularly caring for the superior expression on his face, she turned her eyes away and continued to search for her aunt.

'Damn,' she swore under her breath, 'how can this be happening?' Cora Newcomb had written that this semitropical land was the nearest thing to heaven, the pot of gold at the end of the rainbow. And now she, Molly Rayner, stood alone in a room that was quickly becoming deserted, thinking that perhaps she had been a little hasty in her plans after all. If her aunt didn't show up soon, the promised heaven and gold would both melt beneath the surge of tears she felt building behind her eyes.

3

She drew nearer to the ticket counter, wishing that the tall man with the sarcastic green eyes would move aside a few feet so that he couldn't hear her questioning the ticket agent. He made no attempt to do so.

'Pardon me.' She edged closer, leaning across to speak in a low voice to the man behind the counter.

The man beside her cut his eyes down at her, his lips half curled.

Ignoring him, she whispered to the agent who watched them both: 'Could you tell me if you have a message for Molly Rayner from Mrs. Cora Newcomb?'

'Could you speak louder, young lady,' came the brisk reply. 'I can't hear you.'

She bent closer. 'I'm Molly Rayner from the United States. I expected my aunt to meet me, but she isn't here. Do you know if I have a message?'

A blank expression covered his face. 'You will have to speak louder.'

'Do you have a message from Cora Newcomb?'

The agent shook his head. 'No. No message from Mrs. Newcomb.'

'Are you Molly Rayner?' The tall man grinned down at her.

'You just heard me tell this man my name!' she exclaimed.

A mischievous twinkle suddenly appeared in his eyes. 'If you are Molly Rayner, I'm here to drive you to your aunt's ranch as a favor to her.'

'What?' she asked in awestruck tone. Was he speaking the truth? Had her aunt truly arranged for him to be her mode of transportation or had he merely overheard her telling the ticket agent her plight and decided to take advantage of the situation?

He turned to the man behind the counter: 'Would you have someone load Miss Rayner's luggage in my Jeep? It's parked out by the taxi stand.' As he spoke his hand closed around the handle of her weekender, which was on the floor next to the counter. His eyes came back to her face: 'Shall we go?'

She looked up at him, the fright in her eyes unmistakable and impossible to hide. This seemed to amuse him.

'Come now, Miss Rayner,' he said, straightening his back. 'You're quite safe. My name is Christopher. Christopher Ashburton. My ranch adjoins Mrs. Newcomb's. She would have been here to meet you except for an unfortunate accident.'

'What happened?' asked Molly, concerned and becoming a bit more trustful of the ruggedly handsome man with the strong British accent and piercing green eyes.

'I believe she stepped in a hole and broke

her leg. It was not a spectacular type of accident.' Helping her into the Jeep, he stowed the weekender on top of the luggage already piled high in the back compartment. He swung himself under the wheel, cranked the engine, and they were off.

From the beginning of the trip it was obvious that Christopher Ashburton would not be a talker. Molly watched him out of the corner of her eye; he stared straight ahead, taking little notice of anything but the road in front of him. His skin was tanned and weathered by the New Zealand sunshine, and he wore white cotton pants and a bright green shirt. His hands clutched the wheel tightly; he thrust his lower lip forward as though weighing a great problem.

Molly made no attempt at conversation. Self-consciously she moistened her lips and turned her attention to the town, catching glimpses of one-story wooden houses and a modern little church before the car sped down a block of contemporary office buildings. Tropical trees and huge scarlet and yellow flowers grew everywhere along the drive through the seaside city. She took a deep breath and smiled, obviously pleased with Auckland's quiet, unassuming charm.

'Well?' asked the man of few words.

Startled to hear his voice, she replied, 'Well ... what?'

'You're a stranger here, aren't you?' he asked, keeping his eyes on the road.

Silly question. He knew she was, and he seemed to enjoy taking advantage of the fact. 'Yes, this is my first trip,' she finally answered.

'Is it what you expected?'

Molly paused for a moment before answering meekly: 'It's very pretty.' For some reason she felt at a loss for words. The question had been simple enough, but how could she know what to expect? Only a day ago she had left the cozy apartment that had been her home for three years. Home. Suddenly she felt her chin quiver.

'Are you going to cry?' he asked, flashing a quick smile her way.

'No, I'm not going to cry,' she said stiffly, feeling her face burn with annoyance at him for so easily perceiving her wave of homesickness. Snapping her head around to glare at him, she suddenly began to tremble inside.

With his right eyebrow raised, he wore a thoroughly amused expression on his face. Catching her glance, he winked.

No one had ever made her feel so strange inside, as if something would cut off her breath at any second. Bewildered and confused, she turned to gaze out the side window of the Jeep. The land was certainly beautiful, but she was acutely aware of more than the beauty of this new land.

He drove on a short distance, then slowed and pointed across to a large bay filled with boats of all kinds. 'You must come down to the boat races sometime. It's great fun, if you like boats.'

'I do,' she said, holding her breath, waiting to see if he intended to extend an invitation. Instead he lapsed into silence again.

Suddenly he turned to her, a little impatient. Something irked him, but she certainly had no idea what it could be.

'I must make a brief stop, if you don't mind.'

Before she could answer, he wheeled the Jeep into a long winding drive that led to a lovely two-story mansion situated beyond a cluster of trees.

To Molly, he seemed to jump from the Jeep before turning off the motor. He walked swiftly up the steps leading to a wide-columned porch. She drew a deep breath and watched, thinking how unusual his behavior was, not at all like that of any man she'd ever met.

The door to the large house opened, and out stepped a young woman. She held her body taut, her hand still clutching the doorknob as she talked with Christopher Ashburton. She was a beauty with black hair, dark shining eyes, and smooth tanned skin. But her loud, shrill voice was fit more for a wild bird than for a beautiful woman.

Molly began to feel ill at ease. The Jeep was parked so close to the porch that she could not help but overhear patches of their conversation.

Christopher spoke, his voice barely audible: '... no way of knowing the flight would be late.'

The fashionable woman gave him an incredulous stare, then curled her lips scornfully. 'Well'—she made no attempt to keep her voice out of Molly's hearing range—'you know what this evening means to me. If you can't make it back by eight, then don't bother to come back at all. If taking care of that crazy old woman and her pitiful American schoolteacher-looking niece is more important to you than our plans for tonight—'

Christopher interrupted, but Molly could not understand his mumbling until he nodded and said, '... a few minutes late, but I'll be here.' A moment later he took his seat in the Jeep, his jaw tense, his eyes cold and hard. Taking a handkerchief from his pocket, he wiped his brow. 'I'm sorry for the delay,' he said, turning the key.

'That's quite all right.' Molly cut him short. She looked at him, her long black lashes falling to half-mast over her blue eyes, then added, 'Incidentally, I was a legal

9

secretary, not a schoolteacher.'

He opened his mouth as if to say something, but she turned her face away. She had nothing more to say to him. He was supposedly a friend of her Aunt Cora's. Why, then, had he allowed the black-haired woman to speak of them in such a manner?

Mentally detaching herself from his presence, she turned her attention to the shoreline and watched sea gulls flutter softly over the water. She sat listless, her shoulder-length chestnut hair flying back from her face as the Jeep began to pick up speed. 'Now what is he trying to do?' she asked herself, quickly glancing down at the accelerator. His foot pressed harder, and the Jeep went even faster. Molly bit her lip. It was clear that he placed a greater importance on returning to the big house at the appointed time than on delivering her to Cora Newcomb's in one piece.

'I would like to live long enough to meet my aunt, if you don't mind.' she yelled above the motor's roar. 'I hate to make trips for nothing.'

He looked around quickly. Although he uttered no immediate response, she noticed his foot rising from the floorboard. Then he did an unexpected thing. He brought the Jeep to an abrupt halt in the middle of the road. His eyes moved from her face down to her shoulders, then back to her face again.

'What do you think you're doi—' she began, but he didn't let her finish. She felt the warmth of his breath, then his lips on hers, tenderly at first, then more demanding as his arms tightened around her shoulders, drawing her body closer to his own. Pulling away, she felt a cry of protest escape her throat.

Nothing like this had ever happened to her. Had she not been in a state of shock, she would have been furious at him.

She was aware of his voice: '... and I've never kissed an American,' he was saying.

Uncomprehending, she continued to glare at him.

He shrugged. 'Not bad, I must admit.' He laughed, then continued: 'Kind of a cross between Irish and Dutch, I would say. Closed-mouth and proper.' His eyes glinted with mockery.

She backed against the door. 'You are one hundred percent despicable, Mr. Ashburton!' she said, her voice shaking.

He caught her hand. 'I'd better get out of the middle of the road; I'd hate to have us run down before you get a chance to meet Cora.'

Jerking her hand free from his, she fell back with a sigh of relief as he again cranked the motor. She leaned her head against the seat and closed her eyes, trying to calm herself. Undoubtedly she would never know the answers to a lot of questions she had about this ride. Why the kiss? Why had he met her at the airport? It certainly had been an imposition on him, practically destroying his plans for the evening—and why? He had not offered an explanation except that it was a favor to Cora Newcomb. There must be another more important reason why he had accepted the task of playing delivery boy for her aunt. She fought an insatiable desire to blurt out, 'Who are you, Christopher Ashburton, and what are you up to?'

Feeling the vehicle slow, then turn left at a junction in the road, she opened her eyes. The sky had darkened, the brilliant sunlight fading behind a brief overcast of low grey clouds. The unpaved road wound between bush and fern-covered mountains before crossing a wide plain of green paddocks. To the right at every bend in the road she could catch a glimpse of the sea and sand-covered beaches. The view was one of grandeur.

'Just over the next hill,' he offered without looking her way.

She searched his face; apparently the kiss had been quite forgotten. 'We'll soon be there?'

He glanced fleetingly at her. 'You have been on the Newcomb ranch for the last ten miles—since we turned from the main highway.'

As they topped the hill, she looked down

on a sprawling one-story wooden house painted white. 'It's the first white house I've seen,' she remarked.

'Yes. Most New Zealanders love color. That's why you've seen the pastel-colored houses. My own house is a bright turquoise-blue.'

'Are you a native?'

'No.' He brought the Jeep to a halt outside the house where bright-colored flowers loomed over one another from numerous gardens surrounding the structure. 'You go on in. Don't keep Cora waiting. I'll bring the luggage.' Pausing, he cleared his throat self-consciously. 'I trust you won't tell her I assaulted you. I'd hate for her to lose her good image of me.'

'Don't give it another thought,' she shot back. 'I assure you I haven't been assaulted—nor will I be.'

With a broad smile, Molly alighted. She hesitated a moment before running to the steps that led to the wide front porch. Looking up, she saw an elderly white-haired woman in a loud yellow dress hobble through the doorway, her right leg contained in a plaster cast from foot to knee.

'Welcome, my dear.' The words bubbled with joy, her twinkling eyes mirrored soft, happy emotions. 'I'm so happy to see you at last.' She reached out and grasped Molly's

13

hands. 'Don't move, let me look at you.'
She laughed.

Molly stood motionless, her color rising
as the older woman's eyes traveled across
the small, regular features of her face,
stopping to rest momentarily when they
caught Molly's sky-blue eyes. The young
woman sighed with relief when she heard
her aunt say:

'You are exactly as I dreamed you would
be—young and beautiful, the very image of
the sister I loved so dearly.

Molly turned her eyes away, hoping to
avoid the tears that threatened to come.

Cora Newcomb, her voice trembling,
said, 'I miss her very much, Molly. It broke
my heart when you cabled me she was
dying. I wanted to come and be with her so
badly, but my Phillip, too, lay dying. My
sister and my husband.' She swung around
and fixed her eyes questioningly on
Christopher. 'I told you, Chris, didn't I? I
lost them both within the same week.'

Clutching a bag in both hands, he
nodded. 'Yes, you told me.' He cleared his
throat awkwardly. 'Where would you like
me to put these?'

'Oh, how silly of me,' Cora sputtered.
'Here, bring them inside, by all means.' She
opened the door and waved him in. 'I've
decided she'll be most happy in the east
room. You know the way.' She turned back

and motioned to Molly. 'Come inside, Molly. I know you must be exhausted after such a long trip.' Dragging her right leg, Cora led the way into the large, airy living room with many windows, each one shaded by a wide veranda. The walls were paneled in beautiful grained wood; the sofa and chairs, plush and comfortable, were covered in fabric with large floral designs. Elaborate carved tables, offset by a pale-gold rug, covered the floor. A large stone fireplace stood at the east end of the room.

Molly stood looking first at the splendid room with its calm and quiet atmosphere, then at the large windows overlooking the flower gardens and green lawn. A wonderful sensation gripped her. She stood in darkness, yet the room seemed full of sunbeams; it was quiet, yet filled with beautiful sounds; it was warm, yet cool and soothing.

Christopher Ashburton reentered the room empty-handed. He smiled at the older woman.

'Chris,' Cora said pointedly. 'I thought you'd never get here with her. What took so long? I was beginning to think you had decided to keep her to yourself.'

'The flight was late, Cora,' he returned dryly, glancing quickly at Molly.

Again Molly felt her face flush. How debonair of him to completely ignore Aunt

Cora's last remark. Even though her heart was pounding five hundred beats a minute, she found herself wishing he would go on; she knew he had a hot date waiting on the outskirts of Auckland.

Cora asked anxiously, 'Do you have time for a cup of tea, Chris? I have a kettle on the stove.'

'Oh, no thanks,' he replied, moving to the door. 'I must be on my way. I'll see you in the morning, Cora.' Then he turned to Molly, who had sunk down in a chair near a window: 'I hope you have a pleasant visit, Miss Rayner.'

'A visit!' Cora interjected. 'Molly isn't here to visit me, Chris. She's come to live with me.'

Molly caught the startled expression on his face. He looked like someone who had been slapped, the color rising, then draining. He hesitated, almost spoke, then changed his mind and disappeared through the door.

Molly listened to his footsteps on the porch before allowing herself to look out the window and watch him drive away. She rose and walked over to her aunt. 'He's a strange man, isn't he?'

'Oh, indeed,' Cora replied softly. 'The strangest man you'll most likely ever meet.'

'Why is that?'

The faded blue eyes lit up. 'I'm too old to

16

understand the ways of young people, Molly'—her voice became wistful—'but that young man is a man of great means. I understand his parents are of royal descent. The duke and duchess of—of—, I forget their titles, but anyway, Chris attended the finest schools in London, Vienna, Paris.'

'What in heaven's name is he doing here?'

'Raising cattle. His property adjoins mine on the west line.'

'Do you raise cattle, Aunt Cora?'

Cora Newcomb winced, then laughed. 'Oh, no, my dear. Phillip and I raised sheep for forty years. I suppose I still have close to a thousand breeding ewes and nearly three thousand sheep in all.'

'I didn't see any sheep,' Molly exclaimed. 'Not one.'

'That's because they're grazing the west pastures; you and Chris entered from the east.' She smiled. 'Sit down, dear. I'll bring you a cup of tea, and we'll begin to get acquainted.' A moment later she returned with a silver teapot and cups on a tray.

As Molly sipped she listened attentively to the comments of her aunt. Cora Newcomb was a vast mine of information. She talked first of family ties in the States, then of the North Island, the manners and customs of the inhabitants of the island, and how it had changed since her arrival forty years ago. She talked on and on. Finally she struck on a subject that caused Molly to flush and twist in discomfort.

'And what do you think of young Chris?' Cora asked, a sweet smile playing about the corners of her mouth.

'Why ... wha—what do you mean?' Molly stammered with trembling voice, feeling the rich color flame in her cheeks.

'He is the finest young man. So full of ambition.' Cora laughed happily. 'Why, I wouldn't be surprised if someday he didn't own this entire island.

'He didn't strike me as being particularly overambitious,' retorted Molly with wide blue eyes. *Ambitious* certainly wasn't the word she would have used to describe Christopher Ashburton, but then, she wasn't too sure what word would have been appropriate.

CHAPTER TWO

In her room that night, with only a tiny shaft of light coming through the window, Molly turned restlessly on her pillow, tugging awkwardly at the top sheet, drawing it close about her chin. She could not forget Christopher Ashburton's kiss, nor could she erase the cruel remark overhead outside the mansion near Auckland: 'Pitiful.' For the

18

first time in her life she had been called pitiful. Though she had never thought of herself as being exceptionally beautiful, she had been sought after by several young men in Pennsylvania, but always when the word *love* entered the relationships she had pulled away, clinging desperately to her dream definition of love. Love had not come to her in Pennsylvania. Would she find it in New Zealand? She wondered, filled with doubt.

She felt lonely and bewildered, curious to know what he had thought of her. Again she turned restlessly, her whole body warming as she recalled the touch of his lips on hers. God in heaven! She knew that he had not kissed her because of any warmth or admiration he felt toward her, not because he thought her to be lovely or desirable. She knew that had it been any other young woman from the United States he would have done precisely the same thing. He had explained it quite clearly. He had never kissed an American. She was not going to dwell another moment on his action; she would not permit such disturbing thoughts. She turned her attention to the room.

Becoming accustomed to the darkness, she could dimly make out the objects in the room: bedside table with a vase of fresh flowers placed in the room earlier by Cora Newcomb, the hand-carved dresser and chest, the television, the antique clock on the mantel, ticking away the hours. She sighed, hearing over and over the shrill voice on the porch calling her pitiful.

Did he agree? Did Christopher Ashburton think she was pitiful? She sat up suddenly and threw back the sheet. Remembering his touch stirred her strangely and sent her thoughts wandering back to the afternoon again.

She heard footsteps approaching her doorway. It had to be Aunt Cora; she could hear the cast dragging along the polished wooden floor. She didn't want to let Aunt Cora know that she was still awake. Lying down again, Molly closed her eyes. The door opened slowly, softly; a beam of light fell across her chest, which was rising and falling in rhythmic motion. The door closed, and she heard the footsteps drag on down the hall.

Again she thought of Christopher Ashburton. Closing her eyes, she imagined how he would look in a tuxedo at a gala party, leaning against the bare shoulder of the raven-haired woman. A woman whose hair was too black, her eyes too piercing. She was still thinking of the unlikely pair when she drifted off to sleep.

*　　　*　　　*

Molly was standing at the window in a

white terry-cloth lounge coat when Cora Newcomb opened the door balancing a small tray with a single glass of tomato juice on it.

'Good morning, dear,' Cora said brightly, placing the tray on the bedside table. 'I hope you like tomato juice.'

'Yes, I do,' Molly answered, walking over to the table. She picked up the glass and sipped the ice-cold juice. 'It's perfect, thank you.' She was hesitant to look at her aunt. Her eyes felt heavy, her face was pale.

'How did you rest, Molly?'

Molly smiled at the buxom, matronly woman. 'Fine, thank you, Aunt Cora' she lied.

'Are you ready for breakfast?' Cora asked, appearing somewhat dubious about the last remark.

'Oh, don't go to any trouble; I usually just eat a piece of toast and drink a cup of coffee.'

'Merciful heaven, child, you'll need more than toast and coffee to keep you fueled up in this land. Don't you feel invigorated breathing this fresh air? Now, I'm going to cook you a good American breakfast, and I don't want you arguing with me.' Her eyes went over Molly's slim figure. 'You're not the type to gain weight, and you'll be starved by the time you get back, anyway.'

Uncertain, Molly asked, 'By the time I get

back? Am I going somewhere?'

Cora beamed. 'Me and my big mouth. I have a surprise for you, but I'm not telling until after breakfast.'

'Surprise? What?' Molly asked, puzzled.

'I'm not going to say,' Cora returned after a slight hesitation, 'but I will tell you to dress in slacks.' With that, she turned and clumped off in short steps, apparently well adjusted to the heavy cast.

Molly watched affectionately as she left the room. After gazing out the window at the rolling hills and low blue mountains, she decided to dress.

She wore a pair of close-fitting khaki jeans and cream-colored pullover that reached to her hips. She belted the pants, then combed her straight shoulder-length hair. For a moment she thought about applying makeup but decided on just a touch of rouge for her naturally smooth cheeks.

She studied herself thoughtfully, a fleeting streak of disappointment suffusing her eyes. She was no match for the glamorous, worldly lady she had seen yesterday. Oh, well. She sighed. What possible difference would it make.

Molly came into the kitchen just as Cora placed on the small breakfast table a huge plate covered with fried bacon, sausage, scrambled eggs, and hash-browns. 'My Lord, Aunt Cora,' she protested. 'Surely

22

you don't expect me to eat all that! There's enough food here for Cox's army.'

'I know, dear,' Cora replied calmly. 'But Chris may be hungry. He's due here any minute now. You go ahead and eat while it's hot; don't wait for him.'

'Chris?' she asked reluctantly, hoping the quick flutter in her heart didn't reveal itself in her voice.

'Yes. He's my surprise. I wasn't going to tell until after breakfast, but he's taking you on a tour of the ranch.'

Molly slid down into her chair, placed the napkin across her lap, and picked up a fork, holding it loosely. She cleared her throat. 'Uh ... doesn't he have his own ranch to look after?'

'Of course,' Cora replied crisply, placing another plate on the table. 'But he has his hired hands, a dozen or more.'

Molly heard the Jeep on the dirt road leading to the house. A moment later the motor died. She heard the front door open. He didn't even knock, she thought to herself, just walked right in like it's his house.

His tall figure angled through the doorway. He was wearing a red and blue plaid shirt, a pair of jeans, and polished leather boots. He smiled charmingly at Cora, his flashing white teeth a contrast to his tanned face.

'Morning, Miss Cora,' he drawled, mocking the American cowboy. He turned to Molly: 'Morning, Miss Mol-ly.'

'And a very good morning to you, my Lord Ashburton,' she returned in a clipped British accent. It was an impulsive, half-joking remark, and it never crossed her mind that it would offend him—not until she saw his expression change.

Thankfully, Cora intervened: 'Sit down, Chris, your breakfast is ready.'

'I am hungry,' he admitted, moving to the table, all the time eyeing Molly sharply. Suddenly he yawned. 'Excuse me, I'm still half-asleep.' He yawned again. 'Hurry with the black coffee, Cora.'

'Here,' Molly said abruptly, rising from the table. 'Let me get it. Aunt Cora might not be able to get it to you in time.' She left him staring after her in disbelief.

When she returned, he seemed more alert, though his eyes showed definite traces of little or no sleep during the previous night.

Cora joined them at the table for coffee. They all sat silent for several seconds before she said, 'Be sure and show Molly my sheep, Chris. You know they're in the west pastures.'

'How well I know.' He shook his head and straightened his long legs under the table, brushing against one of Molly's soft-soled casual shoes.

She jerked her foot back.

'About a hundred of them were in my east pasture this morning. Briscoe said a portion of the fence is down.'

'Oh, those animals! They just won't behave themselves. They have all that pasture to graze, and look at them—over there eating up your grass.'

'I told Briscoe to drive them back and mend the fence. We'll check on it while we're out this morning.'

'Do I need to prepare you a lunch?' Cora asked.

'Oh, no, that's not necessary; we'll be back before noon.'

The morning sun blazed down on them from a cloudless blue sky. Christopher Ashburton drove impetuously away from the house, barely giving Molly time to wave to Cora, who stood on the veranda, before they bounced off down the hill. He drove recklessly down the steep road between folding hills, then straight onto a dark sandy beach. Swinging the Jeep around, Chris drove southward.

'This is beautiful!' Molly said blissfully as she viewed the landscape. She knew instinctively that she would love living with Aunt Cora in the white house set in the midst of such beautiful scenery. Taking a deep breath of fresh ocean air, she felt invigorated.

'Can you stop, Christopher? I would like to walk at the water's edge if you wouldn't mind.'

Without replying, he pulled the Jeep to a stop. 'Only for a few minutes. I promised Cora to show you the ranch, not just the beach. You have beaches in America.'

Molly felt the blood rush to her cheeks. She was glad her back was to him so he could not see her face. She jumped onto the sand. Why was he being so antagonistic, as if somehow he resented her presence? But why? What effect could her being here possibly have on him? He wasn't a relative of Cora's. It was all so confusing, his meeting her at the airport, now touring her over the ranch ... Taking off her shoes she placed them on the floorboard and walked out toward the sea, her bare feet not even indenting the hard sand. The air was still and warm.

She felt his presence behind her, then heard him clear his throat.

'Have you every heard of the toheroa?' he asked.

'No. What is it?' she asked.

'Something like a scallop; it's a very famous shellfish and it's only found on certain beaches in New Zealand. This happens to be one of them.' He continued on easily: 'Toheroa is a great delicacy with a unique flavor. It makes a delicious soup or it can be fried or boiled. You see that hole beside your left foot?'

She looked down at the little round hole in the sand and nodded.

'There is a toheroa buried under there.'

'Can we dig it up? I'd like to see it.'

'No. They can only be dug in July and August. It's an ugly creature with a long tongue and a thick white mussellike shell.'

'I just want to see one. I'll let it burrow right back into the sand. I promise.'

He studied her a moment. 'All right.' He spun around, went back to the Jeep, and returned holding a wooden spade. 'Nothing of metal may be used, and only those with shells over three inches long may be taken,' he continued maddeningly, as if he were reading from a textbook. He passed her the spade.

She looked bewildered, suddenly aware that his sea-green eyes were looking down into hers; his lips turned upward in a cunning smile. She took the spade and thrust it toward the sand. It practically bounced back at her. 'This is like concrete,' she sputtered, standing motionless.

He threw back his head and laughed. 'Now, perhaps you would like to continue our trek through this wilderness.'

She looked at him exasperatedly.

From the shoreline he drove inland,

27

rocketing, crashing along a rough dirt road and raising an unbelievable cloud of dust behind the Jeep. Hitting a rut, he nearly threw her bodily over the front window. She grasped the iron bar over her head and steadied herself in the seat. Don't worry, friend, if we become airborne, I won't utter a word. Go on, have your fun.

'Are you enjoying the view?' he yelled, glancing at her.

She remained silent, staring slowly and deliberately at him. Her eyes traveled from the top of his profile and the dark hair blowing loosely in the wind, to the broad shoulders, the muscled arms, and came to rest on the hands curled around the steering wheel. Firm hands, smooth hands, hands that for some reason unnerved her. These hands definitely did not belong to a rancher. She could see his body stiffen under her persistent glare, his superior composure tighten.

A mystery existed about this man, and she intended to find out more about him if she returned to her aunt's in one piece.

'Would you tell me what you are doing?' he suddenly blurted out.

Molly shrugged.

At that moment the Jeep jolted and began to grind strangely along the rough road. Quickly he pulled to a halt and crouched under the wheel, shaking his head. For a second she wondered if something had happened to him.

Then he turned and looked at her, his green eyes holding hers steadily. Again he shook his head. 'I'm afraid we have a flat, Miss Rayner.'

He looked so genuinely disturbed that Molly felt somewhat to blame for the predicament. 'Can I help?' she asked.

'I daresay you can't,' he told her, alighting from his side and staring down at the left front wheel.

Getting out, she walked around to his side. 'I can change a tire,' she offered.

'So could I,' he shot back, 'if I had a spare.'

She looked up at him wide-eyed. 'You mean we don't have a spare?'

Sighing heavily, he leaned against the Jeep. 'That's exactly what I mean.'

'Can we walk?'

'Do you have a better suggestion?'

'How far are we from the ranch?'

'About five miles.' He glanced at his watch.

'What time is it?'

'A quarter past eleven.' He stared at the tire a moment longer, then shrugged. 'I guess we'd better start.' He pushed away from the Jeep, then turned and gave the tire a swift kick.

Molly's blue eyes regarded him in his fit

of temper. A smile played across her lips, but the expression on his face told her to keep the smile inside.

Not a breath of wind stirred as they began the walk through the North Island hill country. It was a challenge to keep up with his long legs; she took two steps for his every one.

The road skirted the hill land, and the view was beautiful. It was such a peaceful land, its vastness slightly frightening. She wished for time to stop and pick some of the bright-colored wild flowers that clung to the hill slopes. However, she dared not slow her pace. If she stopped long enough to pick flowers, she was sure that Christopher Ashburton would walk off and leave her.

A low distant rumble of thunder sounded from behind. Molly stopped and stared back at the heavy clouds gathering behind them, then looked into the disgusted face of Christopher. 'The rain's a long way off, isn't it?' She tried to sound cheerful.

Christopher, his cheeks flushed from the heat, stopped dead still. 'Yes, about five minutes.'

'What will we do?'

He gave her a dry smile. 'Guess.'

The rain came down, blotting out the hills, the trees, the flowers; everything became an indistinct blur. Unable to see ahead, she stopped in her tracks.

'Christopher!' The rain was crashing down with a fury that frightened her. 'Christopher!'

'I'm right here,' he finally answered.

'Can't we find shelter?'

He was silent for a moment. 'It'll end soon. Come on, we'll be on the ridge in a minute. There's shelter below.' He pulled her arm, which upset her balance. Her feet slipped from under her, and she fell to her knees in the muddy road.

'Can't you stand up?' he asked curtly.

A cry escaped her, and then she clamped her teeth together to suppress another wail.

Grabbing her shoulders, he pulled her up roughly. Despite herself, that same tingling warmth spread throughout her body, even though his fingers pinched her skin. Impulsively she shook free of him.

He smiled a crooked, half-mocking smirk at her, then said, 'I was only trying to be helpful.'

She calmly replied, 'Thank you, but I don't need your help.'

The rain slowed, and she could now make out his sulking expression through the fine mist. Pursing her lips, she tromped along the puddled road. He made no attempt to catch up with her.

A few minutes later they stood on the rise above a valley filled with acres and acres of pastures and thousands of sheep. She stared at the sight in amazement. 'My goodness!' she exclaimed, her hand going involuntarily to her mouth. 'My goodness!'

He walked up beside her and looked down in silence.

She watched him closely. A look had come to his face, a look that gave her a flash of intuition.

His eyes swept the pastures restlessly, and a nerve twitched in his left cheek.

'You don't like sheep, do you?' she asked casually.

'Very clever,' he remarked, looking startled. 'A very clever assumption, indeed. But then, I find most Americans to be assuming types.'

'Americans!' She stared at him. 'I never went anywhere with an American who didn't have a spare because he *assumed* he wouldn't have a flat. I never went anywhere with an American in an open-topped vehicle who *assumed* it wouldn't rain!'

There was another silence. 'In case you're interested,' he broke out at last, 'there is a camp nearby equipped with food and a truck.'

She cut him short: 'I'm interested all right. I'm interested in anything that will get me back to the house.'

He shrugged, turned his back, took a few steps, then halted. 'Are you coming?'

'Yes,' she replied gloomily.

A few minutes later, around a bend in the road, they came upon a small weather-beaten shack with one end of the porch tumbled down. Molly couldn't have been happier if it had been a castle on the Rhine. The sun breaking through the clouds made her uncomfortably hot and conscious of leg muscles she hadn't used in an age. 'Is anybody here?' she asked tremulously. 'I don't see anybody, or a tru—' She spun around. What had he done! Here she was in an isolated place in an isolated corner of the earth with a man who had begun the day fresh and clean but now looked like a wild creature, his face red, his hair plastered to his head.

He must have read her mind, for he blurted out, 'You needn't be frightened of me, Miss Rayner. I assure you I have no untoward intentions. I expected Cora's hired hands to be here ... er ... I have no idea where they could be. I didn't see the truck near the pastures. Did you?' His eyes widened quizzically.

'No, I did not,' said Molly, taken aback by his outburst. 'But I will tell you this: I'm not worried! The way this day has gone I wouldn't be surprised at anything!' She inhaled deeply. Hearing something in the trees to her right, she became motionless.

Clear bell-like tones from a single bird above them rang out loud over their heads.

She listened, looking up to the trees. The song came again, even louder. She continued to search the clump of trees for the bird that remained hidden to her eyes.

She looked out over the peaceful North Island countryside, breathing the fresh sweet rain scent into her nostrils. A strange emotion ran through her, giving her heart a new kind of lightness. It was a moment that could make her forget the disastrous events of the morning; it was a moment that could let her look up at the disgruntled man and smile.

'Is something funny?' Christopher asked somberly.

She shook her head. 'I was just listening to that songbird. What is it?'

'Sounded like a tui,' he returned knowingly.

She listened again for the bell-like tones. Instead she heard the roar of a motor in the distance.

'At last!' Christopher sounded relieved. 'I hear the lazy rascals.'

She turned in amazement to look at him. He had sat down on the porch edge and was taking off his boots.

'They're both a hundred years old,' he explained, working his toes back and forth. 'One of them, Sam, is an old Maori warrior, so don't act shocked if he seems a bit strange.'

'Maori?'

'Island natives.'

She liked the quiet enthusiasm always present in his eyes when he spoke of New Zealand. He had a deep affection for this land and its culture, which was obvious to her. 'Are Maoris still around?' she asked.

'Very much so. However, they have reformed somewhat in the past hundred years.'

'Really?'

'Indeed.' His eyes brightened. 'At one time they had a most undesirable diet. One that caused the white man great pain.'

'What?'

He chuckled, arching his brows. 'Guess.'

Molly suddenly became aware of the two men crawling out of the truck. Both wore khaki shorts and shorts; one was definitely Anglo-Saxon, with fair skin and white hair. The driver was a short, dark-skinned man who seemed to crouch with each step he took in their direction.

'Hello, Christopher,' the light-skinned man called out. 'We passed your Jeep.'

'Hello, Jonathan. Hello, Sam.' Christopher rose from the porch and stood in sock feet on the wet ground.

'*Pakeha.*' Sam muttered a greeting. 'Your tire. It is ruined.'

'I know. I need to borrow your truck. I need to get the young mistress back to the

35

house. Cora will be worried.'

Sam turned beady black eyes on Molly: 'You are the girl from the United States of the America?'

'Yes,' Molly replied in hushed voice. 'I'm Molly Rayner.'

'Is good. Is good you come. I tell your aunt she is old woman. Soon will die. Then who will pay Sam for watching the sheep?'

'Sorry, Sam,' Christopher broke in with a laugh, 'you'll have to discuss business some other time. Are the keys in the truck?'

It was very hot in the truck. They motored along the road beside the pasture, the sweltering air filling the cab. They topped a western slope, which opened out into a wide vista, in the middle of which sat the large white house.

'Thank goodness,' Molly whispered. She was thirsty, starving, and filthy.

After a long silence Christopher spoke. 'I do apologize for this morning, Molly. I've been wondering how I might make amends.' He cleared his throat. 'Would you like to come into Auckland Saturday night? There's a dance at the Boat Club.'

She nodded, her heart pounding. Had she really heard it: He had asked her to a dance? This was an invitation he had extended, not one arranged by Aunt Cora. Not wishing to appear overeager, she hesitated a moment, then replied softly, 'Oh, yes, I would love to go.'

'Good. I'll arrange an escort for you. I know a young man I think you will like.'

'Wha—oh.' Molly flushed a deep crimson.

For the remainder of the ride home she made a sincere effort to be honest with herself. Of course it didn't matter, she insisted finally, knowing, as she did so, that she lied.

CHAPTER THREE

It had been only three days since her arrival in New Zealand, and nothing could have prepared Molly for the first two days. She had never thought about meeting such a man as Christopher Ashburton, and she certainly didn't know what to think now that she had. She didn't believe in love at first sight, or even second sight for that matter, but he was definitely the most disturbing man she had ever met, and she felt incredibly weak whenever she recalled the kiss that took her so by surprise. But she was not inclined to think of him in any way except as ... disturbing.

Molly said nothing to Cora Newcomb about the incident, nor could she bring herself to say anything about the awful invitation to the dance. It was a relief when Cora did not mention Christopher's name over breakfast that third morning, for she was a little wary of how she would handle herself in front of the aunt she was growing to love. Somehow she felt Cora would find an excuse for Christopher's behavior, and that realization was an unwelcome one. She had no idea why Cora was so fond of the British Don Juan—but obviously she was very fond of him.

Cora poured more coffee into Molly's cup, then said, 'You're so quiet this morning, dear. Is something wrong?'

With her aunt looking right at her face, Molly wondered how well she concealed her thoughts when answering: 'No. Nothing is wrong. How could anything be wrong in a place as beautiful as this?' She turned her head and stared out the big kitchen window at the magnificent sloping countryside already lighted by a bright morning sun. She sat in silence, still mulling over the cruel trick Christopher had played on her. What did he get out of it? What did it matter to him whether she went to a silly dance or not? He already had his pick of Auckland's society, she told herself morosely. He was under no obligation to find Cora Newcomb's 'pitiful' niece an escort. Why had he done it? She blushed thinking how she must have looked when he volunteered to be an escort for her. Why?

'What are your plans today, Molly?'

Molly looked up questioningly. 'What?'

'Do you have any plans for today?'

'No.' Molly shook her head. 'None.'

Cora sighed. 'Well, we'll have to fix that.' She paused. 'Now, let me see ...'

Molly stared at her in dread. She could read her aunt's mind. She said hurriedly, 'I thought I'd look around myself today. There's so much of the ranch I haven't seen.'

'I'll call Chr—'

'No!' Molly jumped up. 'I'd really prefer to go alone if you don't mind, Aunt Cora.' She saw that Cora sat watching her with a disappointed expression, and for a moment Molly felt guilty for the abruptness in her voice.

'There's a truck and a car in the garage, or there's horses in the pasture. I'd be glad to go, except for my leg.'

'I'll be fine.' Molly smiled, then added, 'I think I'll saddle one of the horses.'

Aunt Cora raised her eyebrows. 'Will you be all right, dear? Horseback riding can be dangerous.'

'I've been a member of a riding club back home since I was old enough to climb into a saddle, so don't worry.'

'Okay. You go get dressed and I'll have Sam get the horse ready. If you'd like, Sam can accompany you.'

'No thanks,' Molly answered quickly. Reluctant as she was about Christopher, she was even more so about having the grumpy old Maori warrior along. 'I'm sure he'd rather be with the sheep.'

'Ah.' Cora laughed, throwing up both hands. 'He'd rather have his rusty old buttocks in the shed twenty-four hours a day.'

'I have the feeling he doesn't approve of me, Aunt Cora.'

'I know,' Cora admitted blandly. 'But I wouldn't give it a second thought. I've been here forty years and he still has not approved of me. You know,' she added with a frown, 'my Phillip's the only person he's ever approved of—but he did worship Phillip. I suppose that's why I keep him around.' She paused. 'Don't get too far from the house, Molly, until you know the land better. It would be easy to get lost.'

'Don't worry, I'll be careful,' Molly replied reassuringly. 'I'll be back in a little while.'

She dressed in jeans and a soft nylon jersey shell for the morning's adventure. Brushing her hair, she tied it at the back of her head with a ribbon. Sitting on the side of the bed, she kicked off her slides and pulled on the boots she had owned since she was fifteen, making a wry face as she

40

struggled.

She walked from the back of the house, then across the yard, toward the barn and the paddock, carrying a wide-brimmed straw hat that Cora had insisted she wear to protect her from the hot morning sun. Rather than argue with her aunt over something as trivial as a straw hat, she had accepted it with a soft thank-you.

Sam cornered a black mare in the fence corner between the stable and the pasture. Cautiously he placed the saddle on her back. The mare's big eyes seemed to be regarding him warily.

Molly noticed the black ears pricked forward and the right front leg pawing the ground.

Sam did not acknowledge her presence in any way, but she was intensely aware that the horse did. At last she spoke: 'Thank you, Sam. I am grateful for you taking the time to do this for me.'

'No thank,' Sam returned dryly. 'Miss Cora she say "Saddle the horse, Sam," so Sam saddle the horse.' Stepping back, Sam wiped his hands on the rear of his trousers.

There was another silence, then she said, 'She looks kind of high-spirited. Is she?'

'Yes,' Sam replied without hesitation.

At that moment Molly had the queer feeling that Sam had arranged for her demise and probably had a pot boiling over an open fire nearby.

Advancing toward the shiny animal, she looked closely at the big eyes. 'Hello, pretty girl,' she whispered, putting out a friendly hand. 'Are you a good girl, or are you going to try and kill me?'

The mare tossed her head and gave a whinny of protest. Molly jumped back.

'Sam! Sam, what have you done!'

Molly winced. She almost wished she had climbed in the darn saddle and let the mare throw her clear to Australia. It certainly would have been more desirable than turning around to face the owner of that curt voice.

Strong hands gripped her arms as she felt herself being pulled back, away from the mare. Through the thin jersey blouse she could feel the warmth of his body against her back. Again the wild sensuous pleasure of his closeness racked her being as she felt the tenseness of the chest muscles pressed against her back. She allowed the strong fingers to stay coiled around her arms until the throbbing pulse in her neck lessened, then she turned slowly and looked at him.

He was looking at Sam, the green eyes filled with anger.

Sam merely returned the glare, the expression in his eyes saying that he felt he had done nothing wrong.

'You   saddled   her,   Sam;   now,'

Christopher commanded, 'you ride her.'

Sam's small black eyes widened with a flash of panic. He shook his head.

'Would you rather I tear your worthless head off?' Christopher asked coldly. He was still gripping Molly's arms, holding her tight against him, moments longer than necessary for the sake of safety.

She had been trying to speak from the moment he grabbed her, but his warm strength possessing her body silenced her voice, leaving her unable to utter a sound. Finally she pulled herself free and stepped forward. Leaning weakly against a fence post, she began, 'Don't hurt him ...'

'Don't hurt him! Haven't you got any sense!' His voice was harsh with anger. 'Do you have any idea what would have happened if you ...'

'I'm sure Sam didn't mean me any harm,' she whispered, her heart racing so hard she felt it would explode at any second.

At that, Sam's large, work-rough hand opened into the air. 'No.' He shook his head, bewildered. 'Sam not hurt Miss Cora's American girl. Miss Cora say she know 'bout horses. Sam give her the finest horse, that's all.'

Christopher spoke with a note of warning in his voice: 'Don't ever do anything this stupid again, Sam.' He nodded his head southward. 'Get on to the sheep!'

With that order, Sam scurried away.

Christopher looked at her in silence for a long moment, his hands tightly clenched at his sides, his eyes blazing at her furiously.

She returned the look rather nervously, seeing the sternness in his face, the harshness making his lips tight and cruel-looking. 'Christopher, I—'

'Don't say anything,' he interrupted contemptuously. 'If you think no more of Cora than to risk your life just to show up a ranch hand, then please be so kind as to keep your explanations to yourself.'

Without another word, Molly turned and started to walk back to the house, torn apart by an emotion she could not identify. She had taken only a few steps when she felt him beside her, stalking in long steps to match her own. Still she felt his anger, but she dared not look up to meet his cold unrelenting eyes.

'Cora means a great deal to me, as does this land. There is no one like her.'

Molly stopped dead in her tracks. 'Cora Newcomb is *my* aunt, but from your actions one would think she's *your* mother! Tell me—why? And when you've finished, tell me what you're doing here in the first place. Aunt Cora didn't mention you coming over today.' She was trembling, her hands shaking in despair. On the verge of tears, she clamped her lips together firmly.

He snorted but did not answer at once.

She looked at him with uncertainty. Obviously his anger was spent for the moment, and his green eyes met hers steadily.

'Cora has been my friend for years.' He gestured, sweeping the air with his hand open. 'While you were living in Pittsburgh—'

'Philadelphia,' she corrected.

'All right, Philadelphia. While you lived not knowing she existed it was I who looked after her. I have checked on her every day since Phillip Newcomb died. It has been I who have sat down with her every morning for tea, who have taken her to the doctor when she was ill, who took her to get her leg set. And all this while you never gave her or this land a thought!'

'So!' Her voice was heavy with emotion. 'You're angry with me because you've had to take care of my aunt. Well, you don't have to do that anymore. I'm here. I'll take care of her. So now you should be happy. It seems I've lifted an awesome burden from your shoulders. Is that why you were worried that I might get hurt—that you would be back playing nursemaid? I guess nursemaid is a bit of a step down for a lord—or whatever the devil you're supposed to be!'

He inhaled deeply. 'Talking to you, Molly

Rayner,' he said quietly, 'is a waste of my good breath. Good day.' He started to walk away, then paused. 'Be ready at seven Saturday. By the way, your escort will be Russell LeDuke.'

Molly stared at him, unbelieving. 'Can I expect him to be as nice as you?'

A slight smile tipped one corner of Christopher Ashburton's mouth as he hesitated, looking at her for a moment. Then he turned and walked away.

She watched as he walked past the house, climbed into the Jeep, and drove off. It was a temptation for her to scream after him in a voice so shrill it would burst his old crazy tires. She resisted the urge; instead she kicked the ground with her scuff-toed boots.

She had coped with everything very well in her short life, had coped with loneliness and tears and disappointments. But she had never before coped with a Christopher Ashburton.

CHAPTER FOUR

'I can't understand Chris,' said Cora Newcomb, shaking her head. 'Of course, I know you're being truthful, but it's so hard for me to understand why he's acting this way. I'm very much vexed by his behavior.'

Molly rubbed her wet hair vigorously with the towel. 'Well, I have nothing to compare his behavior to; he's been quite an ass from the onset. The most difficult person I've ever met.'

Cora Newcomb smiled. 'He certainly does have a commanding personality, doesn't he? My first recollection of him was when he was a lad of about ten years old. He came up to me unexpectedly one day when we were mustering sheep. Such an intent child. His father had just purchased the land north of here when Chris walked up to Phillip and me and wanted to know what price we could charge him for our ranch. He's always wanted this land. He had the biggest, brightest eyes I had ever seen. Even then, he struck me as being a special person.'

'What did you tell him?' Molly asked, feigning disinterest.

Cora leaned back on the plush sofa and looked past her niece with dreamy, unseeing eyes. 'Phillip,' she answered softly, 'Phillip told him that the land was not for sale, but if it ever was, we would let him buy it. He visited us often for a few weeks, then he left and we didn't see him again—Phillip never saw him again—until he returned about four years ago. He had purchased the land from his father and returned here to live. I remember it was a lovely mellow day, everything had a misty look, and I saw him walking up the rise. Even from that distance I knew it was that same little boy. I knew he had come home.' Again she smiled. 'You know, Molly, not everyone falls in love with these islands, but those who do can never leave and stay away. Chris found this out, but he's not satisfied just to live here. He feels he must build an empire. Some type of father-son rivalry, I suppose.'

Still drying her hair, Molly looked wistfully out the window into the darkness. Cora Newcomb thought Christopher Ashburton to be a dear, sweet ambitious boy grown into a dear, sweet ambitious man. She stirred in her chair. Dear, sweet man or cold-blooded, calculating brute. She had come so close to really liking him; her blood grew warm even at the casual mention of his name. I must be feebleminded! she thought, biting her lip. How can I even think of liking him after all he's done and said!

*   *   *

The morning of the dance Molly awoke with a yawn and a mental protest against the coming night. She sat up in the bed and caught a fleeting glimpse of her frowning, disheveled self in the dresser mirror. She tried to force a grin, thinking that if she had to spend the entire day preparing herself for the evening, the time would not be spent in vain. She intended to have Christopher Ashburton's attention.

A glass door opened from her room onto the veranda where a blood-red sun was rising above the horizon, throwing sharp points of light across the porch. Molly sat motionless, her arms around her knees, watching the morning panorama unfold itself beyond her door. The world seemed very still at that moment.

Getting out of bed, she walked across the room, pushed open the door, and went down the steps and out into the garden. Starting at the steps, hydrangeas and rhododendrons planted close to the low foundation of the house spilled out into the nearby bush where big, scented lilies bloomed. The garden was enclosed by a wooden fence, and a stone path wound in and out among the brightly colored flowers to a small weather-stained bench at the far end. A heavy vine sprawled along the fence and tumbled over on the other side.

Her mind carefully reviewed his actions earlier in the week. He had purposely allowed her to believe that he was asking her to the dance for himself, then had played the dirty trick. She should have refused when he mentioned arranging an escort for her, but that, indeed, would probably have satisfied him. He would have known by her refusal that she had been disappointed by the turn of events. Disappointed that it was not him.

A strange feeling came to her as she walked in the garden, vainly trying to sort her thoughts. Although the entire matter irritated her unreasonably, she felt in her heart, without knowing why, that the night could be used to her advantage. It might not be the night she dreamed of, but then, it might not turn out to be the night he dreamed of either.

Early in the evening as she was getting ready for the dance, Molly fought back the waves of ambivalence that swept over her. She had two dresses that she felt were especially suitable for the occasion, but couldn't make up her mind which one she preferred. She finally decided on the clinging, floor-length pale-blue gown that shimmered like silk when the light touched it. Backless, and cut low in the front, the bodice was edged with narrow wisps of lace.

Zipping the dress, she surveyed herself in the mirror from top to toes. She definitely was not the svelte, sophisticated type Christopher Ashburton seemed to prefer, but she knew she looked her very best. Her dark hair gleamed, and she felt transformed, radiant, experiencing a thrill of anticipation.

Sitting down at the dressing table, she

applied makeup carefully, not masking the natural glow of youth and health. A faint hint of eye shadow gave new depth to her light-blue eyes and to the long black lashes, which curved upward naturally. She pulled herself up from the table, knowing she had dressed with extraordinary care–as if everything hinged on this night.

'Dear?' Cora stuck her head in the bedroom. 'Are you ready? Chris is here.'

'Chris!' She couldn't believe it. A fluttering began at the base of her stomach. 'Why is he here? I didn't hear him drive up.'

'He's using the limousine; it doesn't make a noise like that old Jeep.'

Molly's hands were trembling. Just knowing he was in the house played powerfully on her nerves. 'Is he alone?'

'Of course. No need for Russell to drive way out here with Chris living so nearby.' Cora smiled knowingly. 'Russell LeDuke is a very nice young man and I know you'll like him. Chris couldn't afford to make Lydia Frazier mad; otherwise, I feel sure that he would have escorted you himself.'

'Lydia Frazier?' Molly asked, concealing her sudden frustration behind a veil of indifference.

'Oh, yes,' replied Cora sweetly. 'That's the girl people are saying Chris will marry.'

Molly emerged from the bathroom.

'You look very pretty, Molly. Very pretty,

51

indeed.'

'Thank you, Aunt Cora,' she replied quietly. 'I guess I'm ready.'

Seeing Christopher Ashburton in the parlor, she stared at him wide-eyed, her lips parted in surprise. The green eyes with a hint of laughter in their depths caught hers, and he smiled. She felt her heart racing madly as she found herself looking rather helplessly into his eyes, so clear and appealing.

She had never seen a more handsome man. White ruffled shirt, white coat, dark-blue trousers, and tie to match. He looked too perfect.

'Good evening, Molly.' He flashed another brilliant smile and rose from the chair; his eyes taking her in, an eyebrow shot up. 'You look different from the last time I saw you. Been riding any wild horses lately?'

'No, I haven't,' she said rather shortly. She didn't particularly trust that raised eyebrow. She watched him approach, his long legs moving with a natural sureness.

He seemed to study her steadily, as if trying to make up his mind about something. 'Let's go,' he said quietly.

Molly's heart was hammering hard by the time he opened the door for her to slide into the long sleek black car. She could not imagine what this night would be like. She felt so small with him standing beside the door and looking down on her in a steady and terribly disturbing way. Raising her eyes, she met his look as best she could, then looked away.

'Get your dress in,' he ordered coolly.

Grabbing the long skirt, she carefully arranged it around her legs before he slammed the door; he then walked around to his side and slid into the seat beside her.

She opened her mouth to speak, but swiftly and quite unexpectedly he leaned across, placed his hands on either side of her face, and kissed her, forcing her lips apart with a sudden fierce hardness, robbing her mind completely of every emotion except a wild excitement. Then as quickly as he kissed her, he released her, moved back under the wheel, cranked the engine, and drove away from the house.

She drew a deep breath, her lips still warm and tingling, half-parted in sheer surprise. Her throat felt constricted; still she murmured, 'That really wasn't necessary.'

He gave her one brief glance, then turned his eyes back to the road. 'Well, don't flatter yourself into thinking it was. Sometimes I'm a bit impulsive.'

Her blue eyes looked across at him challengingly. Her voice was as low as she could make it and still be sure he would hear her: 'I would call that an understatement,' she whispered nonchalantly. She was proud of her self-control.

'Come now,' he laughed, 'are you going to tell me that you didn't want me to kiss you? From the time you walked into the room you wanted me to. Now, didn't you?'

'Whatever gave you the idea I did?' she returned with a hint of a smile. She spoke faster. 'Tell me about the escort you have lined up for me.'

He frowned, saying nothing for a while. Clearly puzzled by the sudden change in the conversation, he kept his attention on the winding moonlit road. Finally he sighed. 'Poor Russell.'

Glancing at him, she ventured, 'Why do you call him poor Russell?'

'Because he's such a nice fellow, and nice fellows finish last. Don't you agree?'

She stared at him unbelievingly. 'Why would I believe that? Does your philosophy apply to girls? Do nice girls finish last?'

He smiled, and she almost smiled with him. It was so difficult to think clearly while sitting so close to him. Remembering the touch of his lips brought a flush of color to her cheeks and made her peer hastily out the window into the night. He seemed to have the gift of reading her mind.

Russell LeDuke was a man in his early thirties, light, blond-haired, good-looking, with soft brown eyes. He was well poised, graceful, precise, and immaculately dressed in a cream-colored suit, cream-colored shirt, and dark-brown tie. Molly could tell by his appearance that he, too, was a man as highly educated as Christopher Ashburton.

'Glad to see you finally made it, Chris,' called Russell as the two of them entered the club. 'I've almost had to put an arm hold on Lydia.'

Christopher looked around. 'Where is she?'

'Out on the terrace. A couple of idiots are having a bit of a race, and Lydia and some of the others are outside watching for the crack-up.' Then he turned his attention to Molly: 'Hello,' he said, smiling broadly. 'You're Molly?'

'Yes. Hello,' said Molly, feeling somewhat uneasy.

'Would you like a drink?' Russell asked. 'Let's sit down, and you tell me about yourself.'

'Better watch him, Molly,' Christopher interrupted. 'After you tell about yourself, he wants to tell about himself, and believe me, that'll take the entire evening.'

'Evening!' Russell threw back. 'My good man, it'll take at least a week.'

'Excuse me,' Christopher said. 'I've heard it all before.'

Molly watched as he made his way across

the room and out onto the terrace. There was nothing to do but follow Russell LeDuke to a reserved table near the dance floor. From where she sat it was possible to look out onto the terrace at an angle. At first she could not distinguish him from the crowd, then suddenly he emerged into full view. He was standing with his arm around the waist of the woman she'd seen on the porch. Lydia Frazier. She felt a panic sweeping over her. Cora had said Christopher would marry the woman she saw press against his ruffled shirt.

There were many things about Christopher she detested; his self-assurance, his sarcasm, his scornful treatment of her. Yet there were so many things about him she liked: his eyes, his smile, the way he walked, the briskness of his voice. For sure she didn't detest him enough to enjoy seeing him with that woman.

Russell was watching her. 'Perhaps you'd like to walk out on the terrace?'

She jumped. 'Oh, no, I'm fine here.'

'How do you like New Zealand?'

An expected question, it made her feel more comfortable. 'I love it,' she replied, 'I'm staying with my aunt, Cora Newcomb.'

'Ah, Cora. She's some sweetheart.'

'You know her?'

'Everybody on the North Island knows Cora. Up until last year she raced her own boat.'

Molly's eyes widened. 'I didn't know that! She never mentioned boating. Not once.'

'She's still got her boat out there in the boathouse. A hundred people have tried to buy it from her, but she's not selling.'

'Really!' She couldn't hide her excitement. 'A sailboat!'

'Not just a sailboat—the finest sailboat ever constructed by human hands. I've tried to buy it for myself. I went to see her the day she broke her leg; thought I'd get her while she was down.'

'What an awful thing for you to do!'

He chuckled. 'Don't scold me. Needless to say, my approach didn't work.'

'So that's how she knew you.'

'Yes, I've been there many times, always trying to buy something from her. The ranch, the sheep, the *Rainbow*. I should learn someday she's intent on keeping it all, at least for a while yet.'

'The *Rainbow*? Is that her boat?'

'Yes.'

'Well, I'm glad she didn't sell it. It sounds terrific.'

'I always figured when Cora decided to sell the ranch or the boat, she would let Chris have them; I didn't know about you until this week.'

Molly laughed. 'Well, I certainly am not going to buy them. Heavens, I've worked since college as a legal secretary and court stenographer. I made a good salary, but I'm not wealthy by any means.'

'All Americans are supposed to be rich,' he kidded.

'This is one American who isn't.'

Russell laughed. 'Not yet, but my dear girl, I'm afraid you will be someday.'

'I don't understand—' She didn't finish her response, for Russell had turned his attention to the doorway. The clubroom was getting noisy as the crowd came in from the terrace and latecomers arrived. Christopher, holding Lydia's elbow, guided her to the table where Russell and Molly sat.

He pulled out a chair for her. 'Lydia, this is Molly Rayner,' he said as she slipped into the chair. 'Molly, this is Lydia Frazier.'

Molly spoke first: 'Nice to meet you, Lydia.'

Lydia grinned, turning her eyes to Christopher: 'So *this* is the little drowned rat you told me about over the phone the other night,'

Christopher shrugged and smiled bleakly.

'He was mistaken,' Molly said lightly, 'if he told you such a thing. I was only a little drowned mouse. He was the drowned rat.' Never had she wanted to kick a man's shin, but she desperately wanted to pelt his under the table.

Russell laughed heartily. 'There's a story behind this rat talk.' He turned to Molly: 'Tell it to me. I'm the only one at the table who is in the dark.'

'And you're much better off,' declared Molly. 'I thought we ordered a drink.'

Russell threw up his arm to catch a club attendant's attention.

Molly gazed savagely at Christopher Ashburton. How dare you discuss me with this woman, she thought, hoping his mind reading was tuned in. As she looked at his tanned face her anger vanished. It was as though she could hear the clear tones of that tui bird, feel the soft warmth of his lips on hers. Goodness, she thought, I haven't been here a week yet and this man's already driven me crazy. She noticed that Christopher had a rather strange expression on his face, and she wondered if he, too, was remembering.

'Love.' Lydia spoke to him, and his eyes widened. She slid her arm around his. 'Father is having conferences at the house this week. I think I'll come up to the ranch and stay with you.'

He seemed somewhat uneasy. 'You don't have an assignment this week?'

'No.' She leaned closer to him. 'I'm taking some time off. Those lights, hour after hour, damage my skin.'

'Lydia's a model,' Russell whispered to

Molly.

A model. I should have known, thought Molly. She stared at the fashionable woman in heavy makeup and dressed flamboyantly in a loud floral-print gown with absolutely no back and very little front. Both Christopher and Russell completely missed Lydia's face and neck every time they looked her way.

'Of course, you're welcome at the ranch,' Christopher was saying, 'but I'll be busy part of the time.'

'I know that, love, but think of all the time we'll have together when the work is done.'

Christopher grinned at her and squeezed the hand she rested on his arm.

Swiftly Molly turned her attention to the immense room and scanned the other tables. All the men were impressive in suits, fine shirts, and ties—but not one looked as handsome as the man at her table. She also had to conclude that the loveliest woman was at her table, too. Lydia Frazier.

Lights dimmed, and dinner was served punctually at eight. The first item placed before her was a bowl of soup. The aroma and taste were delightful.

'Toheroa soup,' Russell said, bringing his spoon up to his mouth.

Molly looked at Christopher. 'I thought you said toheroa were out of season.'

He grinned shyly and shrugged. 'They are.'

'Don't worry, Molly.' Russell patted her shoulder. 'The club has toheroa soup year round. They're plentiful, even if illegal.'

Next came broiled trout, then lamb and mint sauce. Molly ate heartily, keeping her attention on the meal and refusing to allow her thoughts to ramble.

Lydia toyed with her food. Finally she looked across at Molly: 'Are you afraid of all these calories, dear?' she asked, smiling insolently. 'To me there's nothing sadder than a fat young girl.'

Molly felt the hot fury rising in her. She hurriedly took another bite before she could say something she might regret.

Leaning back in his chair, Russell said, 'Ah, they're bringing in the pavlova and fruit. You'll love it, Molly.'

The pavlova was a meringue cake tasting something like marshmallow and filled with whipped cream and fruit. Molly tasted it. 'What kind of fruit is this?' she asked Russell.

'Passion fruit, my dear,' he returned throatily, a mock-sinister grin on his face.

Following the meal Lydia spoke to Molly: 'I'm going to powder my nose. Care to come along?' She started to rise.

'No, thank you,' Molly returned.

Lydia paused, sitting back down. 'I

suppose there's no rush. My nose isn't shiny, is it, Chris?'

'No. You look beautiful,' Christopher assured her.

Your nose isn't shining, but your fangs are, Lydia, thought Molly disdainfully.

The soft dinner music suddenly changed to a snappy dance beat. Russell said, 'Come on, Molly, let me see what you can do.' Clasping her hand, he led the way to the dance floor. A moment later the floor was so crowded she lost sight of the table where Christopher and Lydia had remained seated.

'Lost somebody?' Russell asked, his wide lips parted in a teasing but affectionate grin.

Molly shook her heard, twisting her shoulders with the beat.

A few minutes later they returned breathlessly to an empty table. Chris and Lydia were gone. Russell relieved her of any doubt as to their whereabouts.

'Friends dance inside,' he smiled, 'and lovers dance on the terrace. That's why the doors are open.'

'I see,' she returned, pushing her hair away from her forehead. She wanted to look out onto the terrace, but her feminine vanity prevented her doing so. But vanity didn't prevent her from wishing for a quick thunderstorm.

It was well past midnight before

Christopher and Lydia reappeared. The music had slowed, and the floor was taken over by slow dancers.

Russell jumped up when the couple approached the table. 'Come on, Lydia, they're playing our song.' Before she had time to refuse, he grabbed her arm and hustled her onto the floor.

'What's wrong with you?' Christopher asked, sitting down.

'Nothing,' Molly replied between clenched teeth. She was so mad at him she thought she would suffocate, but she would not let him know. Her eyes fixed themselves on the terrible smudge of makeup on his ruffles.

'Have you had a pleasant evening?' he inquired.

'Yes.'

He cleared his throat. 'Would you care to dance?'

It figured. Now that it was time for the music to stop he asked her to dance.

'Could we wait for the next one?'

He shrugged. 'Sure.'

She continued to stare at the spot on his shirt. Obviously embarrassed, he tried to pull his jacket casually over the area, all the while looking toward the dance floor.

Seeing Russell and Lydia coming toward the table, Molly was on her feet. 'I'm ready now,' she said.

They passed the returning couple midway. Molly did not glance at them, but she could feel Lydia's expression.

The music began, and Christopher pulled her slowly into his arms. His cheek, smooth, clean-shaven, pressed cool against hers. She closed her eyes. He had to feel her heart pounding furiously against his own. He must have felt the same beauty of the moment that she felt. Let him whisper something wonderful.

'Molly,' he began softly, 'Russell will drive you home. I'm staying in Auckland tonight. I need to attend to some business in the morn—'

'Don't feel you need explain anything to me, Christopher,' she said quickly. She pulled back from his cheek and looked him square in the eyes. 'It's fine for Russell to drive me home. He seems to be a very fine person. I haven't had the opportunity to thank you for introducing him to me. I do thank you.' Of course, that wasn't what she had wanted to say, but she felt she had said it very well.

Christopher had his arm around her, but he drew slightly away and looked down into her face. She could not decipher the expression in his eyes.

When the dance ended, she slipped quickly from his embrace and walked swiftly to the table. She didn't want him to see her face at that moment, for her mask of pretense had slipped away when the music died.

CHAPTER FIVE

Molly arose at six A.M. just as streaks of light in the east broke across the horizon. She dressed quickly, then hurried from the bedroom and left Aunt Cora a note on the kitchen table that said she was riding out to the sheep camp. Molly, breathing in the fresh morning air, ran across the lawn to the stable.

She hoped a ride in the early morning would clarify her thoughts and bring into focus the reality of what was happening to her. It had only taken a short while for her to realize how unhappy she was at the thought of Lydia Frazier spending the week at the Ashburton ranch. The week, almost gone now, brought to mind severe reservations about Christopher. He had not shown himself on the Newcomb spread since the night of the dance.

With sure hands she threw a saddle on the same black mare Sam had saddled for her a week earlier, not knowing why she had decided to ride that high-strung creature. There were other, more gentle horses in the stables, but she would take her ride on the shiny Arab her aunt called Delilah. She was calm as she climbed into the saddle. Her lips tightened as she slapped the reins gently. Delilah responded instantly, quickening into a rapid trot along the road past the house.

Molly turned in the saddle and glanced briefly back toward the house, then gave a sharp dig with her heels, and Delilah broke into a fast gallop. A cool snappy breeze brushed her face and swept back her long hair. Molly smiled to herself. She felt a sureness, an excitement, a feeling she didn't want to lose by thinking of Christopher Ashburton.

'See, Mister Smarty,' she said softly into the wind. 'I can ride—and I can ride very well!' The loneliness of her voice echoed around her head, and she fell into deep thought. Obviously it was a different situation from what she kept telling herself it was. She could not be flippant about Lydia Frazier's hold on Christopher, nor could she find any humor in Miss Frazier's vacation.

'I can't possibly be in love with him, I won't allow it,' she told herself. To love Christopher Ashburton would be like handing her heart to him on a silver platter for him to do with as he saw fit. He had already humiliated her, made light of her, ridiculed her. She set her lips firmly. He wasn't going to do it again. He was selfish and spoiled, and he was spending the week with a woman who was selfish and spoiled. They made a perfect match.

He had at least been courteous enough to notify Aunt Cora not to expect him for tea this week, but of course he'd be there bright and early next Monday and everything would be all right again. Cora would humor and baby him and make over him as if he were a schoolboy. Well, let them play their childish games.

She topped the rise and looked down on the ramshackle old house that Sam and Jonathan occupied while the sheep were in the west pasture. It was set in the midst of a broad valley of rolling grassland surrounded by smooth sloping hills. She pulled Delilah to a halt and dismounted. Leading the mare by the reins, she approached the house; there was not a sign of life.

Strange-looking wild flowers peeked out from the edge of the building, and Molly wondered what kind of flower would have so little pride as to grow next to such an awful-looking old place. She went up to the front door and knocked. Up snapped the shade on the front window to her right. She spun around to see the face glaring at her through the dusty pane.

The man strode across the floor and flung

open the door, where he stood in trousers and undershirt. 'Is something wrong at the house?' he asked, his voice gruff.

'No,' Molly said. 'I wanted to ask some directions. Did I awaken you?'

'No,' he said, rubbing his eyes. 'You want to come in?' he invited grimly. 'I'll put on a pot of tea if you like.'

'Great,' exclaimed Molly, her eyes sparkling at the ruffled old ranch hand. 'I'd love it.'

With a sigh, he stepped aside and impatiently motioned her inside. He pointed her to a chair.

Sitting down, she let her eyes go over the room while Jonathan banged pans around at the sink. The inside of the house was not as bad looking as the outside. One room, two bunk beds against the far wall. On the top bunk the covers were rolled up and placed neatly on the pillow. 'Where's Sam?' she ventured, knowing the top bunk belonged to the old Maori.

He walked over to the wood stove and placed the teakettle on the eye. 'Sam sleeps at the main house,' he said slowly. 'Has ever since Mr. Phillip passed away.'

'Wha—where?' Her eyes widened.

'In the barn. He cleaned out the loft and made himself a room of sorts.'

Sam wasn't there when she took Delilah from the stall. Or was he? The thought of the old man hanging over the loft watching her saddle the high-spirited mare brought a smile to her lips. She had the feeling she had made Sam's day by riding off into the sunrise mounted on Delilah.

Her eyes stopped on a picture hanging on the wall—an oil painting of a ship at sea with rich coloring and encased in a heavy carved frame. Jumping up from her chair, she walked over and took a closer look at it.

'This is beautiful,' she said, reaching out to touch the frame with her fingertips. 'Do you paint, Jonathan?'

'Oh, no,' he chuckled. 'It was a gift.'

Her hand lingered on the frame. She turned questioning eyes to him. The painting did not belong in this tumbledown old shack. It belonged in a fine parlor somewhere.

'Your tea is ready,' he said.

Almost at once after she sat down, her eyes again wandered back to the painting.

Jonathan looked at her quizzically: 'You think the picture is out of place in this house, don't you?'

Lifting the cup to her lips, she peered over the rim at Jonathan. She sipped the tea. 'This is good.'

He nodded in agreement. 'You want a cake?'

'Oh, no,' Molly replied. 'I'll eat breakfast when I get home.'

Jonathan leaned back in his chair, rubbing his hands together. 'Is that Delilah you're riding?'

She grinned. 'Yes.'

His eyes narrowed. 'Sam told me Christopher Ashburton almost killed him for fetching Delilah for you last week.'

Molly shrugged. 'That scene was quite unnecessary. I don't know why Mr. Ashburton jumped to the conclusion I couldn't ride Delilah. I sincerely hope Sam wasn't offended by Chris—Mr. Ashburton's outburst. As I said, it was quite unnecessary.'

Jonathan smiled and passed a hand through his thinning hair. 'That's the way Chris is,' he said thoughtfully. 'Good chap, but quick-tempered.'

She drew her brows into a scowl. It seemed she could not escape Christopher Ashburton, not even on an early morning ride. The man was everywhere.

Jonathan was watching Molly's face. Lighting a cigarette, he dropped the match into a jar top on the table.

Molly sat staring at the large painting on the wall. She was so absorbed in it she didn't hear what Jonathan was saying until:

'—So Chris gave it to Sam.'

'What!' Molly drew in her breath as if his words had wounded her.

'Years ago when he moved to the island,

Sam and me helped him unpack. Sam liked the painting, so Christopher gave it to him. It was just one of the many paintings he brought.'

Molly sat silent. She closed her lips in a firm line and continued to gaze at the picture on the wall. Her active mind went over and over the colors, the brush strokes, the warmth and love found on the canvas. How much of a stranger was this man? Somehow it seemed that she didn't know him at all. Not at all. She was going over every meeting with him bit by bit, examining everything he had done and said, and there was nothing there to point to him as the creator of that fine painting.

'You like the picture very much, don't you?' Jonathan ventured.

'Not particularly,' she retorted, feeling the color rush to her cheeks. Quickly she looked at her watch. 'Goodness,' she exclaimed, jumping up. 'It's almost ten o'clock! I'd better be getting back.' She headed for the door. 'Thank you for the tea.'

He followed her. 'You can go straight across to the east if you care to ride back along the beach,' he told her with a helpful smile.

'You've been very kind. Thank you.'

By the time she reached the water's edge she had nearly succeeded in clearing her mind of the dismay that seized her whenever she found herself thinking of Christopher. She told herself it was because she had never met anyone like him; he really didn't mean anything special to her. It was just that he was unusual, different. She gave a rueful smile and urged Delilah on. The spectacular view of the sea and shoreline became a blur as the warm fresh wind blew across her face.

She pulled the reins, slowing Delilah to a quick trot. The sun was broiling, and she could feel the heat burning the top of her head and her shoulders. Doggedly she guided the mare while scanning the sight ahead of her.

A large umbrella spread open near the water shielded the hot rays from the two forms sitting close together. The turquoise water rolled over the sand and played at their bare feet. Molly squinted, staring in disbelief.

Pulling Delilah to an abrupt halt, Molly felt a surge of anger and a heaviness in her chest as a bitter emotion swept over her. How dare he bring that woman to this beach! This land belonged to Cora Newcomb.

She saw that Christopher and Lydia were oblivious to her presence. Lydia was leaning close to Christopher's bare muscular chest, and their heads were only inches apart. Lydia's black hair hung limply down her

72

back, and Christopher was toying with the ends. They were brushing against one another rather intimately, talking low and laughing. Suddenly Christopher straightened and looked up. He opened his mouth in exclamation as he looked beyond Lydia. Lydia swung around, her eyes wide.

Molly scanned their faces, her eyebrows raised.

Christopher jumped straight up, striking his head on the umbrella. 'Get off that damn horse!' he yelled, flinging his arms wildly. Reaching upward, he grabbed the umbrella and slung it twenty feet into the sea.

Her heart pounding, Molly said, 'Delilah and I are making it fine. I know how to handle horses.'

'Like hell you do!' He walked toward her, his temper flaring.

'Get off—now!'

'No! Aunt Cora would have told me if Delilah—'

Giving a shrill whinny of panic, Delilah tossed her head, then stood swiftly on her hind legs, her front legs pawing the air with fury. Molly, thrown off balance by the mare's sudden movement, felt herself being catapulted through the air. Falling hard on the packed sand, she let out a cry as she heard another high-pitched whinny. Molly opened her eyes to see the hooves above her head. Stunned, the breath knocked out of her, she could not move. Then she felt someone grab her, pulling her away from the hooves that shattered the sand only inches from her head.

'Get away, Delilah!'

Molly heard the sound of a sharp slap against the mare's hind side.

'Get away!'

Lying with eyes closed, Molly heard the hoofbeats fade quickly from the area. Finally she ventured to open her eyes just as she felt herself being lifted into a pair of strong arms. She pressed her face against the bare chest.

'Is she hurt, darling?' It was Lydia's voice.

'Well, if she's not, she should be after the stupid stunt she's pulled!'

Molly started to open her eyes, to tell him she wasn't hurt, but the swift unexpected violence in his tone sent a tide of exhilaration sweeping through her. She hated herself for actually revelling in this moment of closeness. A second later he placed her on one of the large beach towels, and she slowly opened her eyes, to be met by his fiery green ones.

Hovering over her, he said angrily, 'Exactly what did you mean by doing something as dumb as this! It's not that I didn't warn you about that damned horse!'

She squirmed uncomfortably, rising to

her elbows. 'And I told you that I wasn't having any trouble, not until you started screaming and scared the life out of Delilah.'

'Oh, I see. It's all my fault!'

She inhaled deeply. 'To be perfectly honest, it certainly is! I've been on her since daybreak.'

'And that's your good luck, because at any unusual sound she would have dumped you just as she did here. Lucky for you it was here or your brains would probably be bashed out somewhere on this ranch!'

Molly colored. 'I don't believe you. Aunt Cora wouldn't keep a horse that is so dangerous.'

Christopher's eyes narrowed. 'Cora keeps everything Phillip bought. And that doesn't mean everything Phillip bought was a wise investment. But go on and believe what you wish.' He straightened indignantly, not even trying to be tactful. 'Now get your butt up and I'll take you home.'

She bolted to her feet. 'I wouldn't dream of taking you away from your picnic!' Her temper flared. 'I'll get home the same way I got here!'

A look of disbelief shot across his face, then he threw back his head and laughed. 'Oh no you won't. Because you got here on Delilah's back and by now she's already in the stable. So you better listen to me'—again a tinge of anger. 'It's a good twenty-minute walk to the house; it'll probably take you longer because you'll no doubt get lost. Cora will have all that time to worry about you, since Delilah is back in the stable. She won't know if you're lying dead somewhere or not. Now, if you want to worry her, go ahead and strike out on foot.'

Molly stared at him a long time before she finally said seriously, 'I suppose you're right this time.'

'Well, make up your mind.' Lydia suddenly chose to intervene. 'I don't mean to shorten your argument, but this sun is hot as hell and I'd like to get back to the house, if you don't mind, Chris. There's nothing to protect my hair, since you threw the umbrella in the ocean.'

No one spoke throughout the short drive to the Newcomb house. Molly had parked herself in the rear seat along with the uneaten lunch of the two in the front seat. Christopher drove inland along a rough path. Holding on for dear life, Molly felt sure he was trying to sling her out. She was glad when they came to the rise that took them down to the road leading to the house. 'I'll walk from the drive,' she offered above the motor's roar.

A moment later he deposited her at that exact spot. She jumped out and mumbled a low 'Thank you.'

The enraged Christopher made no reply, and a moment later the Jeep sped out of sight.

Molly walked along the drive in long rapid steps, in haste to walk off some of the fury she felt before she faced her aunt.

Cora met her on the steps and led her onto the porch. She seated herself on a settee and drew Molly down beside her, still holding the girl's hand. 'I was getting worried, dear,' she said softly.

'I'm sorry, Aunt Cora.'

'Was that Chris who drove you home?' Cora asked wistfully.

'Yes.'

'Did you have trouble with Delilah?' she asked gently.

'Not really, Aunt Cora. Not until Christopher scared the horse half to death. Then she threw me.'

'Oh, goodness. You weren't hurt, were you?'

'No. Nothing but my pride.' Molly could feel the tears working their way upward. She felt frustrated. Inept. In spite of the heat she felt herself shivering. The warm front porch, usually calm and quiet in its flowering atmosphere, was charged with angry emotion.

'Molly, there is nothing to be gained by anger,' said Cora Newcomb gently. 'You waste both your mental and physical strength. You're angry with Chris, but the best thing for you to do is analyze the situation and see if he truly deserves your anger.'

'I don't have to analyze it, Aunt Cora! He was rude and ugly for no reason. I had no way of knowing he and Lydia Frazier would be picnicking on the beach.'

'Oh, Lydia was with him?'

'Yes.'

'Well,' Cora said, her voice very low and sweet, 'that throws a new light on the matter.'

★　　　★　　　★

That night after the dinner dishes were finished, Molly took a long tub bath, dressed in a pair of pink shorty pajamas, slipped on her robe, and went into the living room. Sitting down at the piano, she touched the keys lightly, wandering into first one melody and then another. Her heart was deeply troubled. Why did she feel so dejected; why such a blank feeling of disappointment? She gave a wistful sigh as she banged the keys loudly, then stood and moved to the window. She looked out across the star-lit garden and breathed in the sweet scents. A sudden speck of light winked through the shrubbery. A firefly in

New Zealand? She had chased the erratic little insects in Pennsylvania on hot summer nights when she was a child, but she had not seen one once she had moved to the city. She watched it hover among the flowers, blinking its light in the darkness. She watched it disappear behind a bush, then she turned to go to her room.

Cora was standing in the doorway, watching her in much the same manner that Molly herself had watched the firefly. 'Are you feeling better, dear?' she asked, her voice little above a whisper.

Molly actually felt herself relaxing a little. She nodded.

'Would you like to sit and talk awhile before you go to bed?'

Molly looked at her aunt soberly, realizing that she might have hurt her feelings today. 'Let's,' she smiled. Then her eyes caught the paintings above her bookcase on either side of the fireplace. Though she had seen them many times, she now looked more closely at the flaming swirls of blue and luminous green. Both paintings were of the sea, but the one on her right, the one with a sailboat riding rough waves, seemed to warrant her closest attention.

'I'll bet you'd never guess who painted those?' Cora said quietly.

'Christopher,' Molly said without hesitation.

'That's right. How did you know?' Cora returned, openly surprised.

'I saw the painting he gave Sam.'

Cora smiled thoughtfully. 'He wasn't the best artist the world has ever known, or even the second best.' A shadow clouded her face. 'That's why he gave it up.'

'He has to be best.' Molly tried to keep her voice detached, though her pulse had already quickened at the mention of his name.

'Don't dislike him, Molly. He's quite arrogant, I know. He's temperamental and somewhat ruthless at times, but he is such a fine young man.'

'I don't dislike him,' Molly muttered.

Cora's hand suddenly flew to her mouth. 'Oh, my goodness,' she exclaimed. 'I completely forgot to tell you Russell called this morning while you were gone.'

'Did he?' she asked nonchalantly.

'Yes. He wants you to go somewhere with him. Oh, darn, I forgot exactly what he did say.'

'Don't worry about it. I'm sure he'll call back.' Suddenly she wanted the sanctuary of her room. 'I'm kind of tired, Aunt Cora. I think I'll go to bed.'

But Molly went to sit at her own window, where she watched the garden for a sign of the firefly. Not until she heard the clock in the living room strike three did she turn reluctantly away and crawl into the comfortable wood-carved bed.

She bit her lip with sheer determination. I'll spend time with Russell. Perhaps I'll even go into Auckland and get a job. I'm not going to waste my life over a man who apparently doesn't care that I exist. She wanted to scream out, 'Do you hear me, Christopher? I'm not going to waste my life waiting for you to look my way. I don't care if you do melt my insides and turn me to jelly all over. I don't care if you are the sexiest man I've ever met. I'm not yours for the asking or yours for the taking.' With that silent outburst, she buried her face in the pillow and wept until she fell into a fitful sleep.

She dreamed of the heaven of finding herself swept into his arms and the hell of being there without his love. She saw herself standing on a mist-covered hill, feeling the beating of her pulses as he moved in a slow animallike motion toward her. She stood motionless, totally helpless as he tilted back her head, entwining his fingers in her hair. He buried his lips against her bare neck, and she quivered with wild sensations. Then he raised his face, and she searched his eyes for the love she knew he must be feeling, and found the green eyes, cold, barbaric. 'Do you love me, Christopher?' she heard herself ask. He answered with a wicked laugh. Heartbroken, she pressed her hands against his shoulders to push him away. He caught her hands and held them firmly, his soft mocking laughter ripping the air.

She awoke abruptly and shot straight up in bed, clutching her head. Bewildered, emotionally drained, all she could do was rub her forehead and utter a faint 'Oh, Lord ...'

CHAPTER SIX

The morning sunlight stirred Molly awake, yet allowed her to lie with eyes closed to the new day. She spent several moments in a twilight existence before the impact of the dream hit her, forcing her eyes open while she lay motionless. She remembered the dream—down to the most minute detail. No longer could she lie to herself; every nerve in her body tingled with the truth.

She loved Christopher Ashburton, and it didn't matter that she told herself she didn't. The dream had conquered her, and in the daylight the taunting knowledge that she did indeed love him frightened her. It frightened her unreasonably to feel a wild passion for a man she hardly knew. Not once had he said a kind word to her; at times he had even been cruel.

She was sitting upright, clutching the bed covers around her knees, when Cora abruptly opened the bedroom door. Startled, Molly pulled the covers up to her neck.

'I'm sorry, Molly, I should have knocked,' Cora apologized, 'but Russell is on the phone. Can you speak to him?'

Molly felt disturbed as she glanced at her aunt. Finally she nodded, then reluctantly crawled out of bed. She walked outside her door and carelessly picked up the hall extension. 'Hello,' she whispered.

'Hey, this is the guy who doesn't extend invitations to just any girl.' A cheerful voice came through the receiver. 'Remember me? Russell?'

She clung helplessly to the phone. 'Yes, Russell, I remember you,' she replied, her voice void of emotion.

'Well, what about our date to spend the day at the club?'

'Wha—what date?'

'Did I mean so little to you that you've forgotten me already, Molly? Was I just a passing flame over your candle? Huh?'

She could see the boyish grin—even through the receiver—as she succumbed to the impish charm. 'Okay, Russell. But I didn't forget; we never made a date to spend the day at the club.'

Russell laughed. 'My dear, that is a trivial

obstacle. I promise you a wonderful day—one you may write in your book of memories.'

Molly felt lighter. 'Good, I need something to put in it right about now. When may I expect this wonderful day?'

'It will begin in about an hour,' came the matter-of-fact reply.

'Today? I couldn't possibly today.'

'Good. I knew you'd agree. See you in about an hour. Bye.'

'Russell!' she yelled. 'Rus—' Too late; he had hung up on her. 'I can't believe this!' she declared loudly.

Cora hurried down the hall, an anxious expression on her face. 'Is something wrong, Molly?'

Impatiently Molly said, 'He's coming here to get me in an hour.'

'Oh, good,' Cora ventured. 'A young woman like yourself needs to be out mingling with the young crowd. I've been worried that you will get bored staying out here on the ranch with me day after day.'

Molly pressed her forehead against the wall near the phone. 'I can't possibly be ready in an hour. I'll have to wash my hair; I don't know what I'll wear. This is impossible.'

Cora wrapped her fingers around Molly's wrist. 'My dear, if God created heaven and earth in seven days, you certainly can wash

84

your hair and put on a pair of shorts in an hour. Don't you think that's possible?'

Without further protest, Molly smiled at her white-haired aunt, leaned forward, and kissed her cheek.

A radiant smile illuminated Cora's face. 'Get busy now; I'll fix your breakfast.'

Turning in the direction of her room, Molly said, 'Don't do that, Aunt Cora. I'm not even hungry.'

'You need to eat,' Cora stated firmly. 'Russell is an active sportsman and he'll wear you to a frazzle if you're empty and malnourished.'

It was useless to argue with her aunt. 'All right, but just pastry and coffee, okay?' She marched into the bedroom, threw off her pajamas, showered, washed her hair, and dressed in thirty minutes. She chose a lime-green terry-cloth outfit: close-fitting shirt and shorts with a wraparound skirt that tied on the side. Regarding herself in the mirror, first without the skirt and then with it, she decided that she had not suffered any loss of weight. It fit exactly as it had in Philadelphia. Taking a piece of ribbon, she tied her hair back from her face.

Russell arrived ten minutes early. He let himself in and found Cora and Molly at the kitchen table. 'Am I in time?' he called from the doorway, then walked into the kitchen.

'Yes.' Cora motioned him over. 'Come

have coffee and cake.' She started to rise, but his hand caught her shoulder.

'I'll get it,' he offered. He winked at Molly. 'Good morning, you pretty girl.'

'Hi, Russell.'

Sitting with Russell and Aunt Cora at the breakfast table, sipping coffee, and listening to them banter back and forth, Molly felt happier than she had in days. Handsome and clean-cut, Russell looked to be what Molly considered a typical New Zealander—light-haired and fair-complexioned. She looked at him long and objectively. He was younger than Christopher, probably by several years. He was as handsome as Christopher in a different way—but he wasn't Chris ...

Suddenly he hit the table and laughed. 'I think I know what you're doing, Molly.'

Wide-eyed, Molly stared at him.

'How about remembering I'm your date. My ESP is at an all-time high today, so be very careful with your thoughts.' He swung around to face Cora: 'May I show her the *Rainbow*?' he asked.

'Of course, Russell,' Cora replied immediately. 'I was going to suggest that you take Molly for a ride if the sea is calm.'

Delighted, he smiled. 'I'll take her out after lunch. You want to come along, Cora?'

'Me?' Cora gave him an astonished look. 'Heavens no. What would I do if we capsized with this thing on my leg?' She hit the cast disgustedly.

★   ★   ★

Thud! Wham! Thud! Molly stood breathless watching Russell retrieve the tennis ball from the far corner of the court.

'You're killing me!' he called across the net. 'Why didn't you tell me you were a pro?' He bounced her the ball.

'I'm not,' Molly replied, standing poised, the ball in her left hand, the racket in her right. She had played an excellent game so far, but she was hesitant to feel too proud at this point. If the next serve was what she anticipated, the match would be hers. She wiped her perspiring brow with her forearm and watched as Russell readied himself.

He stood far back from the net, racket ready, crouching, watching, licking his lips nervously. He was handsome in his blue polo shirt and matching shorts.

She tossed the ball high, striking it with a terrific smash of the racket, driving it viciously across the net, when it suddenly curved unexpectedly and dropped quickly, bouncing three times before Russell realized what had happened.

'You cheated!' he cried. 'Tennis balls aren't supposed to do that!'

Molly curtsied stiffly at him. 'I've always

87

enjoyed playing with a good loser.' She laughed.

He walked over, his arms glistening with sweat, his face wearing the startled expression of the defeated. He mumbled something under his breath.

'What?' she chided good-naturedly. 'I didn't understand you.'

With exaggerated movements he opened his mouth wide. 'I said I only let you win because I felt sorry for you because you're a foreigner in a strange land. If letting you beat me in a game of tennis will help you adapt, then it has been my contribution to your over-all well-being and I am a much better man for having done this generous thing.'

She rolled her eyes at him, then lifted her racket and popped him smartly across his rear with it.

He swung and faced her, his eyes widened with mock indignation. 'Was that a love tap?'

'Call it that if you like'—she raised her eyebrows—'but in the States we call it a swift kick in the butt!' Grasping the ribbon, she untied it and tossed her head. Taking a hand towel from her bag, she briskly wiped her face. 'Could we possibly get something to drink? Watching you run all over the court has made me terribly thirsty.'

'Yes. And because you're such a graceful

winner, I'm going to take you up on the terrace where we can sip our drinks and watch the sea float away.'

'That sounds nice.'

As they walked up the hillside Molly surveyed the beautiful dark-green tree-clad grounds surrounding the rambling clubhouse. Entering the front of the building, they went up a flight of steps and out onto the rooftop terrace, which overlooked the still waters of the bay.

Russell pulled out a chair from the ironwork table near the railing and motioned her to sit. 'This is one of the most beautiful places in the world.' He smiled and pointed across the bay. 'I could sit up here forever and watch the boats come and go.'

Feeling very confused, she looked up at Russell. Heaven help me, she thought, here I am with one man and thinking of another.

'What are you thinking, Molly?'

She shook her head, feeling her chest wall tighten. She needed this friendship with Russell. At this moment she clutched to it as if it were a lifeline to keep her from falling into a bottomless pit of despair.

Russell pressed her hand. 'You want a Coke?'

She nodded, suddenly very close to tears. She sat staring vacantly at the sea below, lost in her thoughts until he returned and casually set the glass of ice at her fingertips.

With an arm stretched to the back of her chair, he leaned over and poured the drink. 'I can add a little something to this if you'd like.'

She shook her head. 'No,' she muttered. 'This is fine.'

'Where did your smile go?' he asked, sitting down, his eyes darkening as he looked at her.

'It's around somewhere.' A deep flush came into her cheeks. 'It seems to be easily misplaced and easily found.' She attempted a weak smile.

'Find it, then,' he ordered. His hand slipped over to her wrist. 'I prefer girls who smile, especially if the girl is with me.' His fingers tightened for a moment, then he released her.

If it had been Christopher's hand ... she thought.

'Do you like the view?' he asked.

'It's very nice.'

'Ah,' he said, tensing, his eyes watching her close. 'Little old ladies are nice, newborn babies are nice, but the view from here is more than nice. I expected something like breathtaking or gorgeous—anything but nice. Come on,' he urged, 'tell me what's eating at you. And don't say nothing, for I am a wise attorney and I know better.'

She met his look. 'You didn't tell me you were an attorney.'

'I didn't tell you what I was; you didn't seem interested enough to ask. I didn't want to bore you when you were obviously much more interested in someone else whose occupation you know.'

'What do you mean?' She was confused.

'You know who I mean. You couldn't enjoy the dance for watching the door. Watching for Ch—'

'Don't say it,' she gasped, clinging to her pride.

'Christopher.' He caught her by the chin and held her face, a knowing glint in his eyes. 'I knew from the moment you walked in the club beside him you were where you wanted to be. Correct me if I'm wrong.'

'Oh, no.' Her smile was sardonic. 'You've said this much, so you might as well say it all.'

He paused, dead serious, 'I hope for your sake you're not in love with him.'

She laughed, a shaky sound in her throat. 'You're being funny, Russell.'

'I hope so.' His wide eyes held hers. 'I really hope so. Lydia Frazier would be more than a little upset to find herself with a rival.'

A sensation of jealousy shot through Molly. That happened to be the one person she had not given much thought. Lydia

Frazier. Little doubt existed that Lydia knew about men; apparently she knew about *one*, with an intimate knowledge. Molly could have found an excuse for Russell's prying if he had kept the black-haired woman out of the conversation, but now she looked coldly and directly into his eyes.

'Of course what Lydia doesn't realize is that you are a rival, regardless of any circumstances.'

'What do you mean by that?' she demanded, fuming.

His eyes narrowed as they took in her angry face, her damp hair, her flushed skin. 'I handle the legal affairs of the Ashburton ranch and also Cora's.'

'You aren't going to be unethical and divulge confidential information, are you?'

'Of course not. But I *will* tell what is general knowledge in this part of the country.' He reared back in the chair. 'Christopher owns ten thousand acres of land, much of it wilderness. Cora owns forty thousand acres of the finest land you will find anywhere on this earth: untouched forests with enough raw timber to build a city, thousands of acres of pasture that could be used for dairying, miles of beaches, acres of citrus, orange and lemon trees, Chinese gooseberries. Of course, the orchards aren't kept anymore but they're still there.' He spoke honestly, frankly. 'If a Garden of Eden ever existed it had to look something like the Newcomb ranch.'

'Why are you telling me this?' Molly interrupted, lifting the glass to her mouth. Underneath she felt shaken by his comments concerning her aunt's property. Undoubtedly Russell was leading to something.

'I want you to realize, at some point Christopher is going to take a real interest in you,' he said with authority.

'You—you don't mean that he'll suddenly develop an interest in me because of Aunt Cora's land?' She was puzzled and angry.

Taking a cheroot from his pocket, Russell flicked his lighter and drew in deeply, his eyes on the flame. Then he spoke, his face wreathed in smoke. 'I don't think it, I know it.' He leaned toward her, holding the cigar away from the table. 'I know Christopher; I know how much he wants that land. He would have married Lydia as long as he thought Cora would eventually sell him the ranch, but you're here now and there's not a fraction of a doubt in my mind concerning the Englishman's new plans.'

Molly sat very still, her palms pressed hard against her face. Russell's revelation was too incredible to believe. Christopher Ashburton openly and obviously disapproved of her. He didn't even display a casual interest. She ran her fingers against her scalp, disarranging her hair.

'I'm not asking you to believe me, Molly.' Russell pressed on. 'I wouldn't do that. I'm telling you what will happen so that when it does you'll be prepared.'

'You're sure of this, aren't you?' Molly asked quietly.

'Yes.' Abruptly he crushed out the cheroot. His smile was cynical. 'You, my innocent darling, will someday be sole heiress to a considerable estate. You are Cora Newcomb's lone living relative. You're not a child, Molly, you can recognize the truth when you hear it.' Suddenly he leaned close to her, and his voice dropped low in his throat: 'Don't harbor foolish hopes about Christopher. You'll get your heart ripped out.'

She dropped her glance. 'I thought you were his friend, Russell,' she whispered.

'Perhaps you'll find it hard to believe, but I am his friend. However, I'm not blind to his faults. When he sets his mind to do something, he does it; Lord help whatever or whoever gets in his way. I applaud his determination. He's come here to build an empire to equal that of his father's in England.' He shrugged. 'And he'll do it, one way or the other. He gave up one dream; he'll never give up this one.'

'You're speaking of his painting?'

'Yes. He studied long and worked hard, and he was good. But he was a rich boy and rich boys play polo in England. He was thrown from his horse during a game and was trampled on quite severely; fractured several bones including his wrist. After the operations and weeks in a cast, he lost his ability.'

A little ache crept into her heart. 'I thought he gave it up because he wasn't good enough.'

Russell chuckled dryly. 'Not good enough! Everything Christopher does is good enough, believe me.'

An hour had flown by since they left the tennis court. Molly sat staring hypnotically into space.

'Enough of this talk,' Russell said laconically, rising slowly. 'Let's go and see the *Rainbow*.'

She rose to her feet and looked dazedly around the terrace, her face very troubled.

The twenty-year-old *Rainbow*, nudged into her berth at the club marina, was indeed a beautiful sail-boat. Twenty-two feet long, she carried a thirty-foot mast. Molly stood on the deck looking at the hundreds of boats docked in the marina, then she looked down at the dark-green bay water, which led quietly out to the vast and boundless sea. 'I think I'd like to go home now, Russell.'

'That might be a good idea,' Russell agreed. 'I wanted to take you out on her, but I see some angry clouds gathering in the west.'

She looked around. A tropical thunderstorm was brewing on the western horizon. The sea gulls diving beyond the boats squawked loud, objecting to the sudden change in wind direction. She suddenly felt a chill.

Russell grabbed her arm, and they ran down the steps to his sports car without saying a word. He pressed the starter, and the motor roared. Backing from the packing space, he threw on the brakes, slung the gear into first, and skidded along the pavement, the wheels screaming.

'I can beat it if I hurry.' He pulled out of the gate of the club grounds and turned north onto the two-lane highway.

Molly caught her breath, then wondered how long it would take her to adjust to traveling down the left side of the road. For a split second she had forgotten she was in New Zealand.

There was no traffic coming. The needle climbed to the seventy mark. As he cut off the main highway onto the side road he clutched down to third, making the right-angle turn at a good sixty miles an hour.

The car bumped along the new road, and

he put his foot down on the gas again, losing control of the car momentarily. Headed straight for the ditch on the right side of the road, Russell did not let his foot up but turned the steering wheel madly to the left.

Molly felt the rear sliding toward the ditch. 'Oh,' she half screamed.

As he struggled with the wheel the slide ceased and they were headed straight in the road again. Slowly he said, 'Sorry, I didn't mean to frighten you, but that will be one hell of a storm when it hits.'

'I would say it's better to sit out a storm than wind up dead in a ditch,' she retorted angrily, looking out at the darkening sky.

He drove at a moderate speed for the next few miles, silent, concentrating on the road that twisted around the low hills. Suddenly it was black dark; Russell pulled on the lights.

Molly sank back against the seat, experiencing a new kind of fright. A loud clap of thunder sounded, and she heard the rain before she saw it splashing on the windshield. Closing her eyes tight, she regretted this day.

CHAPTER SEVEN

In the weeks that followed, Molly grew accustomed to thinking of the sprawling white house as her home and found herself more content as the months passed. It was April and autumn on the North Island; the sultry days had passed as the west wind brought fine weather and clear skies. The gloomy feelings brought about by Russell's talk at the clubhouse had almost completely vanished.

After Christopher's week with Lydia he had flown off to England and had not yet returned. Molly learned from Jonathan that his various ranching activities had been left entirely in the hands of his foreman Briscoe. She also discovered that Christopher had traveled alone; Lydia had not gone with him.

Russell seemed intent on including himself in the inner life on the Newcomb ranch. Although his presence sometimes proved to be a bore, occasionally Molly found him to be rather enjoyable; yet she was never completely comfortable with him. She didn't offer him her best friendship, but she tolerated his presence very well after her tumultuous feelings for Christopher subsided. Even though he was a remarkably handsome man, she could never think of him with real warmth.

She didn't think about love anymore, at least not consciously. She admitted to herself that her secret fears concerning Christopher were not baseless. It occurred to her more than once that this man who was openly hostile toward her could indeed be capable of softening if it suited his purposes. That thought hurt her, and she could not allow herself to cling to it, or else she would find her future to be only an empty abyss. Life at the ranch offered her contentment rather than challenges at the present—but she didn't mind.

The sky was vast and crimson as fleece clouds floated high overhead. Molly swung the truck out of the drive and skirted alongside the sea toward the east pastures where Sam and Jonathan had headed the animals for fall grazing. The seasons would not change as in the States; the weather would remain mild and warm year round, with only occasional drops in temperature.

The sunlight beat hot on the windshield; and so before traveling far, she lowered the window, allowing the wind to brush her face softly. She loved this land, loved breathing in the many fragrances that filled the air. The beauty of the beach drive always filled her heart with a lightness; watching the sea gulls, the bright butterflies that winged inland, the lovely things of color and beauty.

She liked spending the day with Jonathan and Sam and the sheep. There were continuous problems in the pastures; the fencing was old, and every day some of the animals would break out. It wasn't unusual to see dingy white balls of wool as one ambled over a hilltop into the forest or wandered down to the beach on the east side.

Jonathan had bought a good sheep dog in Auckland for four English pounds. The first day after he acquired the pup he realized that it had one shortcoming: It was afraid of sheep. And Sam. Therefore the dog spent most of the day hovering around Jonathan's legs—and Jonathan and Sam chased the sheep.

Sometimes Molly would leave them in the pastures and walk off to the beach and sit alone, hands around her knees, gazing for hours at the rolling sea. Often she stayed away from the house until dusk; she liked going home tired. It was useless to argue or protest with herself any longer. She discovered that when she was tired she slept more soundly.

On one bright April day she was staring at the water when she caught the sound of footsteps. Her heart quickened with hope before she swung around.

100

'What are you doing?' a deep voice rang out.

Her disappointment was evident as she looked up. 'Hello, Russell. How did you find me?'

'I look lessons from Jonathan's dog.' Throwing his head back, he roared with laughter.

She stared up at him solemn-faced.

His bright happy expression vanished. An unusual stillness appeared, and he cleared his throat awkwardly. 'Have you seen him?' he finally asked, a scowl shading his eyes.

'Who?' she asked, jumping to her feet. 'Who?' She could not control her reaction. She clutched his arm. 'Christopher?' she whispered.

'Yes. He's back all in one piece. And I assure you he's his usual self.'

'Where did you see him?'

'I saw him and Lydia in a restaurant.'

Her lips trembled and her face fell to conceal the expression in her eyes.

Russell took her hand and brushed her open palm with his lips. 'I'm not going to allow this, Molly. I need you more than Christopher needs you. He doesn't deserve you. I'm the one who loves you—not him.'

'Russell, please don't say ...'

'I will say it because it's true. I came here today to tell you I love you. I want you to marry me, Molly.'

She could feel the pressure of his hands as they squeezed hers.

'I will not allow you to waste yourself on a man who will only play underhanded games with your emotions.' He gazed down at her, a strange gleam in his eyes. 'You will marry me, Molly.'

She jerked her hands from his, shaking her head. Reluctantly she said, 'Russell, if you spoil our friendship, then we won't have anything.'

'You will marry me, Molly,' he repeated, a smile playing at his lips. 'Remember that when you see him.'

'I'm sorry, but you're wrong, Russell.' Stepping back, she looked him straight in the eyes. The wind blew her hair across her face, and she brushed her forehead, sweeping the hair away from her eyes. 'I'm going now,' she murmured. Retreating back to the truck, she left Russell on the beach staring after her. For a moment she clutched the wheel, strange chills running up and down her spine. Starting the ignition, she sped away without saying good-bye to Jonathan or Sam, and without looking back at Russell.

*   *   *

When she reached the house, she was disappointed not to find his Jeep in the

102

drive. She hastened inside and was surprised to meet Aunt Cora head-on.

If Cora was surprised at Molly's abrupt entrance, she didn't betray it. 'I wish you had been ten minutes earlier, dear. Christopher was here,' she said with a soft smile.

'Was he?' Molly murmured, her heart singing.

'Oh, yes. The trip home to England must have been very satisfying; he looked well and rested.'

Molly stared at her aunt with anxious eyes. 'Is he back to stay?'

'I believe so,' Cora replied. 'He'll be here for tea in the morning; you can ask him yourself.'

'Did he mention me?' she asked as casually as possible.

Cora looked at her strangely. It seemed forever before she said, 'I can't remember exactly what all we did discuss, Molly. We talked about his trip, how long I've had my cast off ...'

'He didn't mention me.' How that simple little statement hurt.

'I think he must have, dear. It's just I can't remember exactly what he said.'

Cora talked on, but nothing more mattered or soothed the hurt.

She escaped into her bedroom, tears flooding her eyes. Throwing herself across the bed, she cried brokenly. She cried until she felt the irresistible urge to kick down the bed.

Her disappointment cut at her like a knife. Would it have hurt him to ask 'How's Molly?' out of common courtesy, if nothing else. How could he hold a conversation with Cora Newcomb and not even mention her niece?

'What have I done to make you hate me, Christopher?' she cried aloud. 'I'll tell you one thing: I don't know how, but someway I'm going to get you out of my system.' Then she added, 'If it kills me!'

A silence lay over the house—a hushed, solemn silence. It was a long time before Molly summoned the courage and strength to leave the solitude of her room and spend the remainder of the evening with Aunt Cora. She found the evening almost unendurable. Aunt Cora did not help the matter with her constant chatter about Christopher Ashburton.

Molly smiled wanly at Cora and asked, 'Did he mention why he went to England?' She really doubted that he had, being the obnoxious, secretive snob that he was.

'No,' Cora replied, 'but he wore a bandage on his right wrist, so I imagine he had another operation.'

'Aunt Cora,' Molly said uneasily, 'Why did you tell me he gave up painting because he wasn't good enough, when all the while it was because of an injury to his arm and hand?' She leaned toward her aunt, waiting for her response.

Cora paused as if concentrating. 'Molly,' she said, 'Chris gave up painting before he suffered those fractures. He wasn't good enough to meet his own expectations, so he quit. Soon after, he was thrown from a horse and did break his arm in several places. That is true. He gave up his skill when he had it, and I suspect that there have been a good many times when he's looked back on that day with regret.' She smiled tenderly. 'He's a keyed-up, determined young man who's headed in thirty directions, not knowing what it is he really wants most.'

Molly stared up at the paintings. Now things were different for Mr. Ashburton. The wildness found on those walls was gone forever. It was as though he had painted the pictures knowing none would ever follow, and all the love, anger, hope, joy, and beauty he felt within his soul he had transferred with a brush onto a canvas and sheltered with a frame.

Molly could feel her aunt watching her, weighing her reactions to the paintings. She felt trapped and resentful, but her irritation with herself lessened as she turned back to Cora.

'You're very fond of him, aren't you, dear?'

'Aunt Cora?' Her voice showed her confusion. 'No, I'm not! I don't even like him.'

Cora leaned back in her chair.

Molly said with a sigh, 'I guess I don't really dislike him.' Standing up, she turned her back to her aunt and walked to the door. 'Good night,' she whispered, not turning around.

'Good night, dear.'

★   ★   ★

Her intentions the next morning were to dress early, pack a lunch, and head out for the pastures, but before she opened the door, she abruptly swung around, declaring silently she would not run from him.

It was a nice warm day with the promise of an afternoon rain. She looked out her window at the soft gray clouds splattered across the horizon. The coming confrontation with Christopher filled her with a mixture of feelings. In his absence she had learned so much about him. So much she didn't understand. The wild allegations from Russell, the quiet revelations from Cora. Which one knew him?

She moved from the window and

undressed. She would not see him this morning in jeans and sweater. She chose a casual navy-blue dress with a thin band of a lighter blue down the sleeves. Standing in front of the mirror, she realized what the dress did for her. Its high collar standing around her chin emphasized the flawlessness of her fair skin, the specks of dark blue in her light eyes, and the sparkle of her long hair. Pressing her hand to the beating pulse in her throat, she wondered how much he would notice.

She heard the Jeep in the driveway. Without looking out the window, she waited until he had time to say good morning and settle himself at the table. She waited in an agony of apprehension; her ears strained to catch his voice. Finally she flung open her door and walked quickly down the hall to the kitchen.

She entered the room.

Christopher half rose to greet her but dropped back into his chair before following through with the gesture. He uttered nothing.

'Good morning,' Molly said in a low voice.

'Morning, dear,' said Aunt Cora. 'Sit down.'

Molly winced inwardly as the silence was broken by Cora—not Christopher. He still had not spoken.

'You're looking well, Christopher.' Molly stood holding the back of her chair, watching Christopher's eyes narrow on her. Cold, hard eyes.

His tall muscular body, in dark-blue suit with open-collared white shirt, looked forbidding, striking. His stillness hovered over the room like a menace.

'How are you.' His brisk tone displayed total disinterest.

'Fine.' She attempted a smile.

His eyes swept over her, moving up and down.

'Tea?' Cora asked, rising from her chair.

'Thank you.' Never had anything hurt her like the expression in those green eyes—sheer contempt or worse.

'You two will have to excuse me,' Cora said quickly. 'I've got to tell Sam ... uh ... I've got to speak with him before he goes to the pastures.' She scurried from the room.

'I'm glad her leg has healed,' Christopher managed to say in a strained voice.

The morning light illuminated his masculine features, and Molly could see his muscular neck where the white shirt lay open. The weeks in England had faded his smooth tan, and the lean face looked pale.

'Are you all right, Christopher?' she asked, indicating the white gauze bandage protruding from his right coat sleeve.

His eyes were intent upon her. 'Oh, it's

nothing much. I'm sure it's nothing to you, one way or the other.'

Her eyes flashed. 'That's right, buster, it's nothing to me.'

His fingers played around the cup rim, and his eyes darkened as he slowly lifted his gaze back to her. Whatever was on his mind could not be fathomed.

'I'm sorry,' he said. 'I don't mean to be rude.'

The atmosphere lightened. She gave him a quick look, and a flush stormed into her cheeks when he faced her squarely.

'How have you spent your weeks, Miss Rayner?' he asked, raising the cup to his lips. 'Have you been bored?'

'Bored?' she echoed. 'No. I've had plenty to do. I've learned a great deal about sheep.'

He seemed amused by the game he played with her.

'Are you going to become a lady shepherd?' His white teeth glimmered in a half smile.

'I've given it some thought; sheep are quite uncomplicated little animals. I like them.' Why not play along.

'I know they're uncomplicated.' He arched his brows and drummed his fingers on the tabletop. 'Like some women—easily led.'

'I would imagine you know.' This time it was Molly who cocked her head at him.

There was a long silence. Finally: 'I must be going.'

'A busy day ahead?'

'Not very. You want to join me?'

Caught completely off guard by the invitation, she gripped the handle of the cup and tried to be steady. How casual. He had invited her to spend the day with him in the same tone that he would have said 'Thanks for the tea.'

Molly hesitated, momentarily startled. She swallowed hard; Christopher's invitation had not been encouraging. Like a good omen, the morning sun shone through the windows, lighting the room with a dazzling brilliance. She felt it warming her back, and she squared her shoulders, taking a deep breath. 'I'd like to,' she said.

'Fine.' He folded his arms and eyed her somberly.

'You'd better tell Cora we may be late getting back; I'm going into Auckland.'

'What?' She stared at his face apprehensively.

'Do you want to go?' he asked briskly.

'Yes,' she said.

Minutes later she found herself looking fleetingly at the countryside as he sped past it. Suddenly he released the accelerator and touched the brake, slowing to a stop at the crossroad. Instead of turning right, toward Auckland, he swung left on a road with great overlapping trees overhead.

'Where are you going?' She couldn't keep the sudden tremor from her voice.

'Home,' he said curtly. 'To get the car. I didn't think of you coming along or I would have driven it instead of this Jeep.' His eyes fixed on hers briefly. 'Is that all right with you?'

'I—I guess so.'

Gradually the Jeep left the forest and traveled on a natural plateau that lay between the trees and the deepening valleys below. The sky had become velvet gray, and Molly realized she had come many miles from her aunt's neat white house with its smooth lawn and flower-scented gardens. Feeling more than a little nervous, she looked over at Christopher; his mouth was set in a firm line. She tried to appear calm.

Christopher pulled the Jeep to a halt. 'This is home.' His voice was strong with feeling, alive with joy.

The large, bright-colored mansion, set peacefully among towering oak trees and giant native bush, was an isolated specimen of beauty. The walls were wood and stone with tall arched windows set deep in the stone.

Again she looked at him with a strange mixture of feelings. She must now show him how touched she was by the magnificent house with its silent grandeur, standing like a stronghold high above the sea. She smiled and shook her head. 'It's beautiful.'

She sat absorbed in the silence and the scents, the warm, powerful vibrant scents of this new paradise. Now that she had finally seen it, she would never forget it. An unexpected shiver ran all through her. She had wanted this ever since she had come to New Zealand—to be in this house with this man.

'Would you like to go inside?' Christopher asked.

'Yes. I'd like that very much.'

A fascinating, magical palace with elaborate furnishings, hand-painted ceilings, and paintings framed in silver, gold, and finely carved woodwork; lofty rich-colored rooms were connected by wide doorways with no doors. Molly looked around, unable to absorb it all in one glance. A great wrought-iron staircase wound along a wall of windows to the left. She climbed the steps, looking out on the wondrous view of sky and below to the rippling dark sea and the restless beauty of the jagged coastline.

Christopher stood below, watching her ascend the stairway, his eyes dark and curious.

'I didn't realize we were so high,' she said, wide-eyed with amazement. 'This house is built on a cliff, isn't it?'

He nodded. 'Yes.'

She stood midway, holding onto the rail. It was an earthy place, a heaven on earth, so different from anything she had ever seen. She looked down at Christopher standing patiently at the bottom of the stairway.

Then his hand caught the railing, and he started up the steps.

Her heart began to race madly in her breast. Slowly he climbed toward her, stopping one step below where she stood. She moved up one step, swinging her gaze to a painting on the opposite wall that was hidden behind a heavy fold of black silk. 'What's behind that drape?' she asked.

He shrugged his fine shoulders and turned, muttering something under his breath. At the bottom of the stairway, he glanced back at her: 'Come on, let me show you the terrace.' He waited for her to descend.

She followed him through the sliding doors onto the marble-tiled floor, which hung over the sloping cliff. The furniture was glass-topped wrought-iron tables with finely moulded chairs to match. She inhaled a deep breath of ocean air and breathed out slowly.

Christopher's hand reached to a chair, pulling it back for her to be seated. Sitting down, she leaned against his fingers, which were still coiled around the chair. She jerked forward—and he removed them. It was a moment of deceit; she could have stayed forever in the small chair feeling his touch on her.

'Would you like something to drink?' he asked quietly.

'Yes, thank you. Anything will be fine.'

He disappeared into the house and returned in a moment with a pitcher and glasses turned down on a silver tray. Methodically he turned up the glasses and poured the beverage.

Absorbed in silence, she tasted the cool sparkling fruit drink. Christopher was leaning against the terrace railing, thoughtfully regarding her.

'How was Lydia yesterday?' Her soft question brutally shattered the atmosphere. She could have bitten off her tongue after the words escaped.

He glared at her, his green eyes stormy. 'Lydia is always—Lydia.'

What did that mean? If only she could retract her foolish question.

He turned on his heels, looking down to the darkening water below, his hands gripping the railing fiercely.

She had not meant to let her womanly emotions show; she did not ever intend for him to see her as conniving, jealous female. She wasn't! Why had she spoken Lydia Frazier's name out loud?

He turned back to her, his face darkly

flushed and tight with an expression she had seen before. 'Lydia doesn't play games.' His voice was low, controlled; his eyes hard and cold. 'Which sets her apart from most women. Wouldn't you agree?'

'I don't intend to discuss Lydia,' Molly returned impatiently. 'Not her virtues, nor her faults. I don't know the woman. I was only trying to make conversation because I knew you had lunch with her yesterday.'

A faint smile touched his lips, and his brows raised quizzically. 'Oh?'

The raising of his brows instantly put her on guard. She reached under the table and straightened her wrinkle-free blue skirt.

He regarded her with the same quizzical expression. 'I'd like to know ... how you knew ... I had lunch with Lydia.' Unemotional, his voice was suddenly austere.

'I don't believe I have to explain anything to you,' she said. A slight frown creased her brow. 'I thought we were going into Auckland.'

He eyed her perceptibly as if fully aware of her reason for changing the subject. Then he pushed himself from the railing and moved toward the glass doors. 'Let's go,' he said coldly.

A moment later he was opening the car door for her.

'Thank you,' she whispered.

They drove into Auckland under skies that were overcast and warm. She silently observed the beautiful countryside with a sinking feeling.

Christopher Ashburton was silent, too, and withdrawn.

'You have a gorgeous home back there.' She attempted to lighten the heavy silence.

He stared out over the steering wheel without answering, a man deep in his own thoughts. She eyed him longingly. He was certainly magnificent, a man alive with physical magnetism. How many months had she been aware of her body's desire for him? Mind over body. Her mind might say no forever, yet her body had its own need, its own yearning—an urge for life.

CHAPTER EIGHT

After a quick lunch downtown Christopher left Molly in a department store while he ran his errand. Thirty minutes later he returned to the store and searched her out of the crowd. He seemed different. He didn't avoid her, he smiled and made light conversation as they walked leisurely to the parking lot.

Traffic was light as they made their way from the city. The sun had broken through

116

the haze, and Christopher switched on the air conditioner. He drove past the tropic trees and twisted bush that grew on the sloping sides of the road. For the first time she felt completely at ease with him. She dwelt on that fact rather than the landscape. Glancing out the window with only a faint interest, she suddenly straightened in the seat as she realized exactly where they were.

The bay was crowded with all kinds of boats brought inland by the earlier threat of storming seas. Several men on sloops were bringing down their large white sails, making the vessels appear like sitting birds stripped of their wings.

A tormenting uneasiness filled her. She glanced toward the clubhouse. Mid afternoon would surely find Russell there. She searched, her head in a whirl. She saw it. She saw Russell's car in the parking lot when Christopher wheeled through the entrance and skidded to a halt.

He swung around, a smile on his lips. 'How about a drink?'

She shook her head.

His green eyes traveled over her deliberately. 'Any special reason why not?'

She tilted her chin arrogantly. 'No reason; I'm just not thirsty.' She said it with more confidence that she felt. She was aware that behind those inscrutable eyes he was finding his own answer.

'I'm going in,' he said, and opened the door. 'Join me if you like.' He walked across the lot toward the building without looking back, almost as if he knew she would follow.

Moistening her dry lips, she sat unmoving. Finally realizing he wasn't going to give in and return to her, she got out of the car and slammed the door.

Entering the crowded building, she spied Christopher at the bar with Russell. Smiling politely at Russell but ignoring his motion to join them, she seated herself at a table in the corner and waited for Christopher to finish his drink.

Thirty minutes later he walked over to where she was sitting and said, 'Are you ready to go?'

Molly was too exasperated to be civil, yet she was afraid to attack him outright; there was something about his expression that told her to tread lightly.

'Did you enjoy your drink?' she murmured dryly.

'I certainly did,' he assured her solemnly. 'Let's go, I want to take you down to the marina where the *Rainbow* is—'

'I've seen the boat,' she interrupted, rising from her chair.

Guiding her toward the door, he returned quietly, 'Yes, I suppose you have, at that.'

As they started back toward the ranch Molly scanned Christopher's features

118

closely, shrinking away from the controlled fury that hid in his face. Slowly the seed of suspicion took root in her mind. He had spent half an hour at the bar with Russell, and she had no doubts about what was discussed. Everything was going wrong now.

He turned to her. 'It didn't take too long for you to find yourself a lover, did it?' He looked at her with contemptuous disgust.

'What did you say?' she whispered.

'You really should avoid little boys who kiss and tell, Molly.' He was suddenly very calm.

The bright flush slowly receded from her angry face, her eyes like blue flames dancing out at him. 'Has anyone ever told you you're a very offensive man? You say so little to insinuate so much. Are you accusing me of having an affair with Russell? Is that what you're trying to say? If so, then say it!'

For an instant he hesitated, then replied, 'I have reason to believe that you and Russell are more than just friends, as you might say. However, he did tell me that he plans to marry you.'

Complete disbelief flooded her. 'I really don't want to talk to you now—or ever, Mr. Ashburton! And the same goes for your very good friend and confidant, Russell LeDuke. Except let's not leave this field of honor just yet. If your accusations were true—which they aren't—wouldn't *you* be the one to sit

119

in judgement on me! How did you and Lydia Frazier spend that week together—playing tiddlywinks?'

Total and absolute silence reigned for the remainder of the trip back to the Newcomb house. When they arrived, it was full night and Molly, disillusioned beyond words, felt terribly tired. Her real sorrow was not that Christopher had accused her of having an affair with Russell, but that he had never opened his eyes long enough to look at her and realize that she loved him.

Loved him. Past tense. For how could she love him now or ever again. The rain fell hard, and without saying a word, she flung open the car door and ran into the house, leaving him behind in the car.

*   *   *

Molly and Aunt Cora, as they often did on rainy days, sat in the quiet living room. They had just finished a game of gin in which Molly, as usual, wound up owing Cora fifteen hundred pounds.

'You will put it on my revolving account, won't you, Aunt Cora?' She tried hard to smile.

'Of course, dear.' Cora said brightly. 'I believe that brings your total debt to just over a hundred thousand American dollars. You'd better watch out or you'll end up owing me as much as Christopher.'

Outwardly Molly tried not to flinch at the mention of his name. Her aunt loved him as a mother might love a very dear son, which at times frightened Molly.

'Which reminds me.' Cora spoke again. 'It doesn't seem that Chris is coming again this morning.' She shook her head. 'It must be the rain.'

Many times Molly had almost reached the point of voluntary confession concerning the events of the day spent with Christopher, but something held her back from tarnishing the image Cora had of him. She had, however, told Cora that should Russell LeDuke ever phone again, she would not speak to him, and should he ever appear on the Newcomb land, she would not see him. Cora had not pressed for an explanation.

At ten o'clock Molly put away the cards and closed the drawer that held the score paid. Just as the drawer shut she heard the Jeep splashing up the drive.

'That's Chris.' Cora's voice filled with delight.

Molly fell silent.

'My goodness, I don't have the tea on. Molly, take care of him while I attend to the tea.' With that, she hurried from the room.

With great effort Molly pulled herself together enough to face him when he entered the room. She met his eyes and said, 'Good morning, Christopher.' Void of feeling.

He returned the look. A long searching look; a look that a few weeks ago she would have given the world for. But now she found it to be quite meaningless.

'Good morning, Molly.' He stood across the room from her.

The door opened, and Cora came in.

Christopher turned and smiled broadly.

'Tea will be ready in a minute, Chris,' Cora said sweetly. 'Now, sit down and I'll bring it in here.' She advanced to the heavy carved table, picked up the empty juice glasses she and Molly had used earlier, and walked back to the door. 'I'll be back in a few minutes.'

The room was very quiet. Molly reached over and pulled the cord on a shaded lamp, which cast a sudden circle of golden light in the corner where it stood. Then she gazed moodily at her feet.

'You haven't told Cora about our argument at the club?' he asked softly.

'No. Why worry her with triviality such as that,' Molly replied bitterly. She felt his green eyes upon her and ignored them until she couldn't bear it a moment longer. 'Stop staring at me, Christopher,' she ordered.

He leaped to his feet and crossed the room in great strides.

'And don't you dare touch me!' she cried.

Ignoring her outburst, he leaned over and tenderly kissed her cold, unresponsive lips. Stepping back, he looked deep into her eyes and smiled tenderly. 'Molly—I—I—'

She glared back at him, unflinching.

'Confound you, Molly,' he whispered, the smile gone.

Cora chose that moment to enter the room with the tray. 'What have you been doing these rainy days, Chris?' she asked, placing the service on the table.

'Taking life easy,' he replied, sitting down. 'Looking after the ranch and doing a little sketching.' He moved his wrist back and forth for her to see. 'This last surgery is successful, I believe.'

'What wonderful news, Chris.' Cora beamed warmly. 'I'm so happy for you.'

Molly rose shakily from her chair. 'If you will excuse me, I have a few chores to do in my room.'

Christopher stood, clearing his throat awkwardly. 'I—uh—before you go, I wanted to invite you and Cora to be my guests Sunday. We're having the annual fall boat races.'

'Dear boy!' Cora actually squealed with delight.

'You must race the *Rainbow*! You will, won't you, Chris? She's still the fastest on the island. I'll bet my hoops on that!'

'Of course. I was hoping you'd offer. I'm afraid she's going to rot sitting there in the marina.'

Casting a cutting look at him, Molly walked to the door. Of course, he would do it willingly, she thought. But anything he did, he had a motive for—just like Russell LeDuke.

Going down the hall, she heard Cora saying, 'I beat Molly at gin a few minutes ago; you want to try your luck?'

'Sure,' he answered, just as Molly knew he would.

★   ★   ★

On Sunday the sun was shining; the sky was blue and cloudless with a brisk westward wind.

Driving along the beach road, Molly noticed the whitecaps that rippled along the surface of the sea, and she wondered if the bay waters would be smooth for the races.

Cora, sitting beside her in the shiny old car and clutching a pair of binoculars, said excitedly, 'I feel wonderful knowing Chris will be sailing the *Rainbow*.'

Molly felt her blood rise, but offered no comment.

A huge crowd had gathered at the club for the sporting event. Already the boats were moving cautiously from the docks into the bay, their sails spread out like wings on silver doves.

Christopher met them in the parking lot and led them to a spot bayside where the view out over the channel was magnificent.

With an onslaught of mixed feelings, Molly watched as the *Rainbow* sailed out to join the other entrants. In every direction there were boats and races to watch.

The twenty-two-foot-long *Rainbow*, with six hundred feet of sail, was in the first regatta. The boats sailed west with the wind.

From where Molly and Aunt Cora sat, the going looked easy. The channel appeared relatively free of hazards, except for the clutter of boats. Molly shaded her eyes with her hand and breathlessly watched the boats racing across the sunlit waters of the bay with sails outspread and flags flowing gracefully as the crowd cheered the vessels on. It was a moment of joy too beautiful to be described.

Molly glanced at her aunt who had the binoculars pressed firmly in front of her eyes. A stream of tears flowed beneath the eyepieces, down the wrinkled cheeks.

'Aunt Cora,' she whispered.

Lowering the binoculars momentarily, Cora said, 'Don't mind me, dear, whenever I see the *Rainbow* out there I get emotional.'

The spectators rose to their feet, waving

and yelling as the boats weaved in and out around one another. Then from nowhere a fast-moving sail drove from the crowd and shot like a bolt toward the *Rainbow*.

'Come on, LeDuke!' a man shouted. 'Steer him aside!'

Her mouth open, Molly peered anxiously as the boats swept faster toward the finish line. They were within a hundred yards when the wind suddenly whipped high, sending the back vessel out of control. It thundered into the side of the *Rainbow*.

Molly scrambled to her feet and ran to the water's edge, her heart pounding wildly. The sun was bright, and a small seagull circled her head as she stood helplessly and watched the *Rainbow* capsize and sink before her eyes. All that remained afloat was the sail.

'Christopher,' she whispered frantically, her eyes searching the water. Then she saw the motorboat approach the wreckage; a moment latter a man dragged himself up from the water and over the side of the rescue vessel. Unable to watch another moment, Molly spun around and ran back to her aunt.

A dazed expression on her face, Cora Newcomb limply held the binoculars in her lap. 'Is Christopher all right?' she asked in a whisper.

'I think so.' Molly swallowed hard,

126

unashamedly letting the tears stream down her face. 'But the *Rainbow*'s gone.'

Molly and Cora climbed a small rise and stood in the midst of small bushes and flowers to watch the accident victims unload. Christopher was the first to climb out of the boat. The tremendous crowd had gathered in close to watch and cheer. Molly had a difficult time following him with her eyes after he climbed up on the pier.

Christopher walked with his head down, his dark hair plastered against his scalp, his drenched trousers and shirt clinging to his skin.

Heartsick, Molly shivered, watching him make his way in and out of the crowd, his eyes downcast. At the terrifying moment of the collision she discovered her feelings for him were still very much alive. The wreck had jolted her nerves and set her mind to swirling with thoughts of what she would do if he did not rise from the water. Her lips had moved in quick prayer while the tears flowed.

Now she watched him approach the end of the pier. She knew finding Cora had been his first thought as his head lifted for the first time since the landing, his stricken eyes searching the crowd.

From out of nowhere a woman, dressed immaculately, darted from the gathering of people and ran swiftly toward him. She threw her arms around his neck. His face, which had been blank and preoccupied, suddenly softened as he took her in his arms and kissed her.

Molly recognized that woman as Lydia Frazier. She watched as they talked, then Christopher kissed her again.

The new feeling of warmth toward him began sinking in Molly's chest, just as the *Rainbow* had sunk out in the bay. 'Let's go home, Aunt Cora,' she whispered.

Cora nodded, wordless.

Together they walked to the parking lot, neither looking back at the bright sails out on the water or the mass of people on the shore. Then a voice cried out behind them:

'Cora! Molly!'

Stopping under the shadow of a tree, the two women turned around. Russell LeDuke ran toward them.

Russell was a mischievous man, and she had known it for some time. Not only had he told lies about her, but now he had wrecked the *Rainbow* in his attempt to outdo Christopher. She dreaded even listening to his voice. Her eyes fell to the ground when he approached.

'I'm sorry, Cora,' he said emotionally, he voice high. 'I'm sorry. I didn't mean to ram her—'

In a small, quiet voice Cora answered, 'I know you didn't Russell. It was an accident.

128

The *Rainbow* was old, but she was a good ship in her day. Don't worry about it. I loved the boat and the man who built her, and I'd much rather see her go out there in the bay, racing with her great beauty, than sitting stagnant and rotting in the harbor. So don't you worry about it.' A graceful silence fell.

It was enough to bring the tears back to Molly's eyes. It was unbelievable that the boat was gone, but even more unbelievable that Russell LeDuke had actually begged forgiveness.

Molly drove home slowly.

That night, after dinner, Molly sat alone in the living room sipping a glass of wine. It was very difficult for her to understand what had happened.

Cora had retired for the evening. Christopher had not come. She wondered what Cora had thought or felt about Christopher's behavior, but her aunt had turned her thoughts inward and there was no way to know what was going on in her mind.

Molly swallowed a gulp of wine, then studied the fragile glass. A knock sounded at the door, and she jumped with a start. She had not heard an automobile on the drive. Without hurrying, she set down the glass and walked to the door. 'Who's there?'

'It's Christopher.'

Her heart did a somersault, and she waited for it to quiet before she turned the lock. Frowning, she opened the door.

He was leaning against the frame, his clothes rumpled.

'What is it?' she asked, staring at him.

'I would like to speak to Cora.'

'She's already gone to bed.'

He considered that statement for a while. 'May I come in?'

An uneasy pause; then she stepped aside and allowed him to enter, feeling resentment for his complicating what had been an uneventful evening.

'I know she's upset,' he began, standing tall and straight in the lamp's glow.

Relishing the chance to be insufferably cool, she interrupted, 'Now's a fine time for you to realize it,' She looked up at the clock; it was after eleven.

'I—I'll be back in the morning to see her.' With that, he spun around and hurried out the door.

After she locked the door, Molly turned off the living room lamp and went down the hall to her room. Inside the bedroom, she leaned back against the door; then crossing the room, she went outside to walk in the moonlit garden.

What a moon! A lovely full moon shone bright in a dark-blue sea of stars. She had the desire to run and run and run. Run out across the sparkling lawn, leaving behind all her heartache and disappointment. But she stood still, clutching a leaf on a waist-high bush. She had seen him, his muscular arms enfolding Lydia Frazier. She protested the thought with an inward cry of rage, tearing the leaf from the bush and flinging it to the ground.

Two feelings tore at her. Secret temptations she had to solve by herself. She wanted Christopher Ashburton, wanted him to want her, but always she found reasons and ways to push him away. She was uncertain and beset by fears.

If she had fallen in love with him, how bitter was this love. Then perhaps she had not fallen in love with him; perhaps the attraction she felt was only physical. One thing she knew: if the feeling was simply brought on by his handsome looks and physical appeal, in time it would most certainly die away. But if she loved him, she knew in her heart that the feeling would never die. She turned and went back to her bedroom.

A blood-red sun was rising when she drifted off to sleep.

CHAPTER NINE

Christopher had come and gone while she slept. When she awakened, there was no impulse to jump out of bed and hurry into the new day. Still, there was a warmness as she lay motionless and looked around the room. She loved all the familiar things in the room and spacious house; now she felt that she belonged to this house and this land.

Getting out of bed slowly, she went into the bathroom and brushed her teeth, then reached across and turned on the bathwater, asking herself what she would do this day. One thing was certain: She had to keep busy.

Molly found her aunt in the seldom-used office across from the living room. She was sitting at the desk, her hands flat on the top. On hearing Molly's footsteps, she straightened. 'Come in, Molly.'

The room, larger than necessary, was paneled in dark-grained kauri pine felled on the ranch by Phillip Newcomb. There were trophy heads and paintings on the walls. Walking slowly around the room, Molly studied them. On the wall behind the desk hung a large topographical map that showed the outlines of the Newcomb land.

Cora said slowly, 'Christopher was here.'

'Did he get everything straightened out?' she asked, trying to focus her attention on the map.

Cora smiled at her. 'Sit down, Molly,' she said. 'We have things we need to discuss.'

Molly walked to the leather sofa across from the desk and sat down.

Cora moved her hands from the desk to her lap. She cleared her throat. 'You've been here several months now, Molly. You've explored most of the land; you've been to Auckland and the surrounding villages. I would say you've had insight into the life here.' She paused. 'Every day you've been here you've been a pleasure to me. I think of you as the daughter I never had; and if you stay, this land will be yours when I'm gone.'

Molly was clearly uneasy. 'Aunt Cora'—her solemn blue eyes widened—I didn't come to New Zealand to get your land. Heavens, when I received your letter I had no earthly idea you owned this ranch. I only knew that you were a relative I had never seen and your letters were warm and inviting. I came here to be with you.' She suddenly stood. 'And if you *were* gone, I don't know that I would want this land. This is big country and I don't know that I could handle it.'

Cora wore an easy smile. 'Yes, it is big

country. I didn't bother to explain it to you in my letters because I wanted to see if your blood ties were strong enough to bring you here on your own.' Her eyes met Molly's head-on. 'Dear, that's why I didn't send you money for your passage here. Did you ever wonder why I didn't even offer, after you arrived and realized that I was financially well off?'

Molly took a deep breath. 'No. I never thought about it. It seemed like a good way to spend some of my savings.'

Cora continued to smile. 'I know you're terribly independent, but then, that's a family trait I'm very proud of. I brought you in here to explain that with the exception of a few relatively small bequests, you will inherit everything.' She paused. 'I had bequeathed Christopher the *Rainbow*...'

Silent, Molly stood looking at the tough little lady sitting behind the large desk.

'That's all I wanted to tell you, Molly,' Cora whispered at last, close to tears.

*   *   *

In a way, Molly thought to herself, I must also have some of the blood that flows through wild creatures who roam the countryside. Instinctively, when she felt lonely or frightened—as she felt at this moment—she sought solitude. Taking the truck, she drove away from the house.

For a time the dirt road led through silver fern and giant tree fern, hedgerows of great blue agapanthus, big hot-country versions of the orange montbretia, and occasional wide sweeps of pale-yellow dunes. Then, leveling off, the road led to the pastures; the scent of the kauri pines filled the air around her.

Stopping the truck before entering the pastures, she got out and began to walk. In the shelter of the pines there was a quiet hush. She crossed a small stream and paused to admire a growth of wild orchids. Further on downstream a small bright-green bush caught her eye. Alone, she felt strangely soothed.

In the United States she had lived most of her life in a city, but she knew she would never return. She had lived in a world of tall buildings, crowded sidewalks, fast taxis, but now she was out of tune with that style of life. She and her college friends had thought that the only life for a young female was to rent an apartment, get a job, mingle with people one's own age, so she had gone to work in Philadelphia. She hated sitting in the office or the courtroom listening to people badger one another, crafty lawyers at play. She had met and mingled with people her own age, with their projects and schemes, but found that she didn't belong as a bustling member of a bustling society.

She had never discussed her feelings with anyone. But someone existed now that she wanted to discuss them with—if he would allow her.

She came on a large fallen tree and kicked the rotten bark with the toe of her boot. Yes, there was someone. Someone who, like her, didn't belong out there in the bustling world.

There had been times when his eyes met hers and she would think, He is falling in love with me! But Christopher Ashburton, with his fierce emotions, had not fallen in love with her. He was only playing games to make her physically aware of him.

Russell, of all people, had warned her to watch out for Christopher. Russell, who had proved to be the most dangerous friend a girl could have. Russell had messed up the only good day she had ever had with Christopher. Kicking the dead tree again, she wished she had the last part of that day to live over. She would march right into the club, regardless of the spectacle Russell made.

It was midafternoon when she got back to the ranch. Feeling drowsy and lazy, she thought about an afternoon nap. Stretching out on the veranda lounger after a ham sandwich and a glass of tea, she closed her eyes and sighed.

With her eyes closed, she reached back

and straightened her sweater. She heard a car on the drive. Opening her eyes into tiny slits, she turned to see who could be calling at this time of the afternoon. She knew Cora was not expecting anyone, or else her aunt wouldn't have lain down for her afternoon rest period.

Her eyes opened wide. She found herself looking at Lydia Frazier, who was emerging from a sleek little sports car. For a moment Lydia, with her jet-black hair, sharp dark eyes, and skillfully made-up face, stood motionless, staring toward the house. She wore the latest fashion in expensive casual clothes, a yellow silk shirt and divided skirt in a vivid print with yellow flowers. She held a pair of enormous sunglasses in her hand.

Molly, in her dirty boots, denims, and worn ribbed shirt, bolted upright on the lounger and swung her feet to the floor.

Lydia gave her a bleak smile. 'I hope I didn't disturb your nap,' she said with an air of haughtiness.

Molly felt herself shudder. 'No,' she said quietly. 'I wasn't asleep.'

'I need to speak with you,' Lydia said dryly, and took a seat in the chair next to the lounger. 'Could you get me a drink of water? The drive was farther than I expected, and my throat is painfully dry.' Her eyes flickered over Molly.

'Sure,' Molly replied, and disappeared

into the house. She came back a few minutes later carrying a tray with one glass of water. She placed it on the low table beside Lydia's chair. 'Would you care for anything else?' she asked, sounding like a waitress.

'No, this is fine,' replied Lydia, who took the glass and sipped the water as if it were the strongest of wines. 'Ah ... I think I'm getting a headache.' She opened her purse, took out a box of aspirins, and delicately placed a couple in her mouth. She took another drink of water, swallowed, and then inhaled deeply. 'Now,' she said, 'how shall I begin?'

'Why not at the beginning,' Molly suggested, trying to help out.

Lydia frowned. 'I see you have a bit of humor, Miss Rayner. But quite frankly what I am about to discuss with you, believe me, is not at all humorous. I've come to tell you to leave Christopher alone.'

Molly bit her lip hard. For that, she had no response.

Lydia raised her brows with apparent disgust. 'For a while there, I just looked on with amusement, because to me, you and Christopher were very amusing.'

Molly's blue eyes darkened.

Lydia sighed. 'But after a while things that start out funny, aren't funny anymore. If you want a man, I would advise you to look for one of your own. I don't know about social mores in the States, but here, nice women don't mess around with another woman's man.'

Molly cleared her throat. 'Excuse me, Miss Frazier, would you mind being a little more explicit? I'm not sure I follow you.'

Again Lydia's brow shot up. 'Oh, you follow me all right. You know exactly what I'm talking about. My Christopher has been through some very trying times, but this thing with that damn boat has almost knocked him off his feet. I've never seen him so distraught over anything.' She reached down and smoothed the divided skirt. 'He won't even speak to me about it. It's all your fault. You and that aunt of yours—I'm sure if you hadn't insisted, he would have sailed his own rig—and won. Now he has all these guilt feelings about wrecking something *special*.'

Molly swallowed hard, fighting to remain civil. 'The *Rainbow* was something special,' she uttered.

Bewildered, Lydia shot back, 'It was a damn old boat! That's all. Certainly not worth the mental torture Christopher is putting himself through.'

'I can't do anything about the *Rainbow*, Lydia. If Christopher is upset over wrecking her, I can certainly understand his feelings.'

Lydia sneered: 'I'm sure you can. Just as

you understand most of his feelings—or so you think.'

Molly breathed rapidly, her cheeks burning. 'You're wrong, Lydia. There's no one on this earth I understand less than Christopher Ashburton. If you believe otherwise, then that's your mistake!'

'Knowing Christopher as I do, I'm confident it won't take him long to gain control of his physical emotions where you're concerned. But that doesn't alter the fact that you're interfering with our happiness, and I want it stopped! I can overlook a few sexual experiences between you because I know he found you to be different—a temptation, so to speak. And men are funny about trying something *new*.'

Molly jumped to her feet. 'Have you ever considered getting together with Russell LeDuke! The two of you have the most overworked imaginations of any two people I've ever met!'

Lydia looked shocked. 'Russell LeDuke is my brother!' she spat. 'Don't tell me you didn't know that!'

'Russell is your brother!' she exclaimed, shocked. 'How would I know that? Nobody thought enough of it to tell me. Your name is Frazier, his is LeDuke, so how was I to figure that out?'

Lydia's eyes widened, reflecting her disbelief. 'Frazier is my professional name; I
140

am a LeDuke. My father is Winfred LeDuke.'

'Well.' Molly's chest heaved. 'I'm not up to par on my mind-reading act. You'll have to forgive me. From the way you said Winfred LeDuke, I suppose I should know *him*, too.'

Lydia controlled herself with outward difficulty. 'He's only the governor of this island.'

'Well, I certainly will mend my wayward ways now. Had I known who you were, I would never have spent all those nights with Chris. But then, we didn't spend too much time in conversation.' She laughed throatily. 'You know how he is.'

'Yes.' Undisturbed, Lydia smiled mockingly. 'I do know. And I intend to keep it that way. Just so you can't squeal "Nobody told me," I want you to know from me that Chris and I will soon formally announce our engagement. You better become a good American and live by your hands-off policy.'

'I certainly will,' Molly said quickly. 'Now that I've heard it from the horse's mouth.' She chuckled low. 'That's another old American expression.'

'I can tell you've found this little chat to be delightful. I'm glad you've taken it so well. It's been my experience that women don't like other women telling them what to

141

do.'

'Oh, I've enjoyed it immensely,' Molly said, biting her tongue. 'But I wouldn't advise you to do it again. We Americans often resort to violence if we feel someone is intimidating us.'

Without saying another word, Lydia jumped up, grabbed her purse, pushed her sunglasses on, and walked smartly down the steps, not looking back.

CHAPTER TEN

Molly watched the car until it disappeared from sight. Totally dejected, she flung herself on the lounger. I'm not going to cry. Let him marry her. I'm not going to cry. All the while, the tears spilled down onto the bright-colored padding. She buried her head in her arms.

Startled, she sensed she was not alone on the veranda. Her head jerked upward.

Cora stood there in her stocking feet, wearing a loose-fitting duster.

'Aunt Cora,' said Molly.

'I'm sorry, child, I didn't eavesdrop intentionally, but I heard Lydia.'

Embarrassed, Molly said, 'You heard her; you heard those things she said to me about Christopher?' She sat upright.

'Yes. And I heard those things you said to her.' Not moving her eyes from Molly, Cora backed up to the chair Lydia had occupied, and sat down. 'I heard you in the kitchen getting the water; I stayed behind the door and listened.

'Why? Why didn't you come out? I'm sure it wouldn't have mattered to Lydia Frazier ... or LeDuke ... or whatever her name happens to be!'

'You're mistaken there, Molly. She would indeed have minded my presence. No, I stayed where I was for good reason.'

'What reason?' Molly's tears had dried, but her cheeks were stained. 'I don't understand.'

Cora shook her head, brushing her forehead with her fingertips. 'I've been here a long time, Molly. Forty years. Phillip and I always wanted to keep this land as pure and clean as we found it. To us it represented the rainbow; not the pot of gold that most people search so hard for, but the beautiful rainbow itself.'

'Is that how the boat got its name?' asked Molly quietly.

'Yes. Many times Phillip and I discussed the loveliness found here. We knew beauty and the importance of beauty in our lives. But we also discovered there is another side of beauty. Take Delilah, for instance.'

'Delilah!' Molly was shaken. She had not

ridden the mare since the day that it threw her on the beach.

'Did you know that Phillip bought her while on a business trip to England? She was a high-strung filly, full of pride. Phillip fell in love with the horse and had her shipped, fully aware that he might never calm her enough to ride her. She was the most magnificent creature he had ever seen, and he wanted her to be a part of this ranch. He saved her life by bringing her here; she was to be destroyed.'

'Destroyed! Why?'

Cora leaned back in the chair. 'It seems she was guilty of throwing her young rider during a game of polo, causing him much injury.'

Molly suddenly paled. 'Christopher?' she whispered.

Smiling sadly, Cora nodded. 'Yes, it was Christopher. So you see, dear, the prize mare that was so dear to my Phillip, the animal he considered to be beautiful above all others, is not a thing of beauty to Christopher. I thought he would pass out with anger when he saw her that first time. Never had I witnessed such hate in a young man toward an animal.'

'Why didn't you tell me this before now, Aunt Cora?' She understood now why Christopher had been so outraged and furiously angry with the mare. It had seemed so preposterous and unjust at the time—but now she understood.

'Delilah is a constant reminder to Chris, Molly, that one does not ever escape his past. It will always find him. I have lived with the hope that someday he will stroke the mare tenderly and forgive her for weakness.' She wore a faraway expression for a moment, then suddenly returned to the present. 'Lydia and Russell have indeed played dangerous games with your and Christopher's well-being, but I understand their motives.'

Molly listened with great interest as Cora began again: 'Lydia and Russell know something about this land that I am quite sure neither you nor Chris suspects.' She paused as if unsure of her next words. 'Have you ever seen an oil refinery or the oil fields in Texas, Molly?'

Molly shook her head. 'Only on TV or in the movies.'

'Have you wondered why Russell and Lydia have been so hell-bent on keeping you and Chris apart? The lies, the stories; first those Russell told you about Chris, then the ones he told Chris about you. Heaven only knows what Lydia's been telling, or to whom.'

'I—I thought jealousy was probably the basis of it.' She shook her head vigorously. 'I really haven't understood it at all!'

'My dear, jealousy doesn't motivate like the power of money.' Cora's face looked older as she said, 'Winfred LeDuke is a proud New Zealander. He's a very influential man, probably the most influential on the North Island. Can you imagine what it does to him to know that a great part of this island is owned by an American and an Englishman?'

Baffled, Molly shook her head again. 'No, I don't know why it would matter to him. Somebody has to own it.'

'Well, Winfred is quite aware of what the world is like today. He lives in a political world; he knows what this land could mean to a rich American oil company.'

'Oil company?' asked Molly incredulously. 'I don't understand.'

'Ten years ago Phillip and I allowed the northern section of our land to be tested by a government survey team. The samples they took for testing revealed a ninety-five percent possibility that beneath the surface lies a rich supply of oil.'

Molly stood up and walked to the edge of the veranda. She walked slowly back and forth beside the wooden railing. Finally she said slowly, 'You mean Russell and Lydia knew about the survey? That's why Lydia's latched onto Christopher and why Russell tried to...'

'Exactly. The eastern section of

Christopher's land would definitely be involved. He's always been very honest and plainspoken, that's why I'm sure he doesn't know. I've wanted to tell him, but I promised Phillip before he died that I wouldn't tell Chris. I can't break that promise.'

Molly's voice was faint and distant: 'Why have you told me, Aunt Cora? What will I do now that I know?'

'You'll do what I expect you to do, or I'll be sorely disappointed in you.'

'I can't tell him,' Molly said gently. 'That's all he's heard since he returned from England. Stories. I doubt that he'd even believe me.'

'I can't tell you how to handle this, Molly. I can't tell you what to say or what not to say. If you are the young lady of judgment I believe you to be, when the time comes you'll know how to handle it.' She rose slowly from her chair and walked to the door, then turned around. 'I consider Chris family, Molly. I love him dearly. That's why I couldn't be too upset with him for wrecking the *Rainbow*. But I have asked myself many times since that race if it really was an accident.' Cora opened the door and walked into the house, but not before she stared a long moment at her niece.

Molly noticed the indelible marks of age lining her aunt's face, the fatigue in her

147

eyes. She tried hard to smile for her aunt, but failed dismally.

After Cora had gone into the house, Molly looked out across the lawn, wondering if she would ever really smile again.

Molly mocked herself: What a complete fool I've been. She could not control her shaking; her every emotion lay torn and bleeding. Dashing down the porch steps, she began to run, tears again blurring her vision. When she reached the back pasture, she turned to the stable. Seeing Delilah outside, near the fence, she stopped.

Delilah pulled up a few blades of grass and stood with her head over the fence, chewing slowly, taking great care not to lose a blade protruding from the side of her mouth.

Standing close to the fence, Molly reached up and stroked the mare between the ears.

Suddenly Molly knew what she must do. Spinning around, she ran back to the house and stuck her head inside the back door. 'Aunt Cora, I'll be back in a while. Don't worry.' She ran to the garage, opened the truck door, and jumped in. There were several hours of daylight left.

She traveled along the road in a haze. She shivered, but not from the cool air blowing into the truck from the opened window

148

vent. She drove impatiently, pressing the accelerator closer to the floorboard. Would she remember how to get to his house from the turnoff?

She gunned the motor, taking the truck up the slope of the narrow road. Looking up, she caught a glimpse of herself in the rearview mirror. She looked horrible. That didn't matter. Nothing mattered except that she see him.

She tried to rehearse mentally what she would say when he answered the door. She felt a knot in her stomach as she got closer to his house. She whispered, 'Hello, Christopher, I came to pay you a neighborly visit.' No! That would never do. Start all over.

She would knock on the door. There would be a pause. He would open the door, his green eyes wide, and he would say, 'Molly! What are you doing here?' Yes, that's what he would say. But what would she reply? She couldn't just walk in and open up with all she knew.

Pulling up in front of his house, she ran from the truck to the front entrance. An awkward moment followed.

She still didn't know exactly what she would say. Her senses told her shaking hand to knock on the door. Inhaling deeply, she realized she still didn't know exactly why she'd chosen to do this. She straightened her sweater.

She knocked again.

A horrible thought crept upon her then. She spun around to see if Lydia's car was parked beside his in the side garage. No. Just his Jeep and his car. She felt the pulse throbbing in her neck.

She knocked the third time. She could hear no sound within the rambling house. Then suddenly she heard his phone ring. It rang again. Again and again.

No one answered. She glanced around the lawn, then turned back to the door. She turned the knob. Unlocked. The door opened.

'Christopher,' she called out in a small voice.

She waited.

'Christopher.' Louder.

She walked inside. The entrance hall was dark. She reached out her hand, steadying herself against the wall. 'Christopher!' Moistening her lips, she moved with uncertainty into the large elaborate room of windows—the room with the narrow winding staircase leading up to the second floor.

Her breathing slowed, and she looked around the room.

Walking over to the floor-to-ceiling windows, she peered outside onto the terrace. No sign of him. A single glass sat half filled on the table. A sketching board and a box of charcoal lay in the seat of a chair. Sliding open the door, she walked onto the floor, her boots clicking against the tile. She picked up the sketching board, and a sad smile played at the corner of her lips. Her eyes focused on the sweeping sea and the small sailboat sketched in on the left side of the paper.

Molly raised her head and turned back to the windows. She looked past the winding steps to a door that stood slightly ajar, and for an instant she wondered...

Shafts of gray-white light slanted through the windows, and she could see the folds of a covering over what seemed to be a painting. Half scared by her own thoughts, she turned back to the sketch.

Where are you, Christopher?

She placed the sketchboard back on the chair.

Where *are* you?

Moving to the terrace railing, she looked down to the coastline. A small rowboat was pulled up on the sand and tied to a rock jutting from the water. She stood, waiting to see if he would appear.

Leaning over slightly, she called down, 'Christopher, are you down there?'

No answer, except the small waves lashing the rocks.

Turning, she went back into the house,

151

sliding the door closed very slowly. Her back against the door, she shook her head, her hair hanging loose over her shoulders. She walked to the foot of the stairs and peeked through the narrow opening in the door that led to a small room. She wondered what was hidden behind that velvet drape in the corner.

She licked her lips nervously.

Slowly she entered the room, taking a deep steady breath before reaching the halfway point. Gradually she approached the object and touched its black covering.

Her reaction bewildered her. She didn't know whether to look beneath the drape or run from the room. What part of Christopher lay hidden behind the silk?

Seizing the velvet, she slowly lifted it.

For a moment she didn't know what she was looking at. It was the portrait of a man. The sunlight shone bright on his hair and well-dressed, muscular body. He held a glass of wine in his hand. Her glance swept over the painting and its magnificent colors, moving back and forth, up and down. But it was a portrait of a man with no face.

She stared at the empty portion of the canvas.

A voice, cruel and clear, rang out: 'Molly! What in the hell have you done?'

She jumped up and faced him.

CHAPTER ELEVEN

'Christopher!'

He came toward her. 'What the devil did you think you were doing in there!'

Molly stood there, unable to speak. What could she say? Was there a defense for her actions?

'Why did you do it?' he demanded, grabbing her shoulders. 'Curiosity? Was that it? His blazing eyes swept her face. 'Tell me, did you find it fascinating? Do you enjoy snooping around in other people's homes?' He leaned closer.

Suddenly her heart leaped, turned around in her chest, and then quieted. Detaching herself from his nearness for an instant, she opened her mouth in an attempt to speak: 'I—I'm sorry, Christopher. I know there is no excuse for my actions. All I can do is tell you I'm sorry.'

His fingers dug deeper into her flesh. She felt an awful guilt and a growing fear as his eyes raged at her, a violent fury flaming behind the green irises.

Unsuspecting, he had walked into his home to find her intruding on a very private part of his life, and now, as she faced him, she had to fear his reaction to her prying curiosity.

Each part of the portrait seemed sharply etched in Molly's mind as she stared wide-eyed and unblinkingly into Christopher's hostile eyes. She knew she was looking at the face that belonged with the well-dressed muscular torso on the canvas. A self-portrait—unfinished. Painted by the artist who could not capture his own expression; the artist who could not see his own face.

The blood at his temples throbbed visibly as the fury mounted. He looked as if filled with the desire to place his hands around her neck and choke the very life from her—and she didn't blame him.

'Christopher,' she whispered. 'Please ... please let me explain what happened.'

'Explain!' he snarled contemptuously. 'Tell me, how can you dare offer an explanation?'

Molly looked at him, her mouth trembling, her blue eyes filled with anxiety. Then she realized that not only was he angry, he was also hurt. She indeed felt herself to be the culprit reflected in his eyes. 'I—I didn't come here to pry. Honestly, I didn't,' she said, earnestly attempting to explain.

Suddenly he released her. Stepping back, he asked, 'Tell me, then, why *did* you come here?' The lines were deep in his forehead; his British accent was much more pronounced. A tall, forceful figure wearing loose-fitting tweed trousers and a sloppy white shirt that hid the ruggedness of his body, he folded his arms across his chest and waited for her reply.

Her feeling of panic was still too great for her to be coherent. 'Christopher.' Her voice choked, and tears sprang up in her eyes. 'I—I only ... I only came here ... to see you ... to talk ...' Her voice failed her, and she shook her head in despair.

'You'll tell me!' Once more brutal fingers bore into her shoulders with such fierceness she cried out, her head spinning as he shook her back and forth. 'You'll tell me! You'll tell me if it takes all night!' He compressed his lips so tightly that a whiteness appeared across them.

Molly passed her tongue over her dry lips, frantically trying to free herself from his grip. 'Let me go,' she cried.

His eyes narrowed. 'Why, certainly I'll let you go.' With that, he released her shoulders and grabbed her by the forearm, dragging her bodily out of the house and down a worn path to the deserted beach where the boat lay tied to a rock. Once out of the house, he seemed less angry. 'You may now join me on my fishing trip,' he said, 'which you so rudely interrupted.'

'I—I can't,' she returned, her voice trembling.

'I insist.' He released her completely and walked out toward the boat.

Sitting down on a nearby rock, she watched him in total despondency. She watched him, wondering what he was doing and why. A brisk cool wind blowing in from the sea chilled her to the bone. He wasn't speaking at all now. He struggled with some fishing lines ignoring her totally. She closed her eyes and listened as the water hissed along the shore, slapping the rocks, then washing back out to sea. Slowly she opened her eyes again and watched him, his hair blowing in the wind. He was handsome, with the fine features of the natural aristocrat. She was surprised to feel her heart beating quite rapidly.

He looked up at her as though startled, as if he had forgotten she was there on the rock. His eyes widened. 'I'm almost ready,' he said. 'Come on.'

'You know I can't go. I've got to get back to the house.'

'Which house? Yours or mine?' he asked, full of sarcasm. Stepping out of the boat, he walked closer to the rock, studying her.

She felt her heart constrict. 'I see you aren't going to forgive my intrusion, Christopher. I told you I was sorry.'

He sat down beside her on the sand. 'All right, Molly Rayner, let's talk about whatever you said you came to talk about.'

He studied her very closely.

'You don't like me very much, do you, Christopher?'

'Should I?'

She looked out over the sea, then up to the scattered clouds, feeling his great intensity, not knowing if he was really aware of her or not. 'Yes. You should,' she finally answered. 'For I like you very much, in spite of your ill temper and bad manners. In spite of those things I still like you.'

He seemed embarrassed. 'Do you?' He turned to her with disbelief.

'Yes.'

A silence fell between them, and Molly could think of nothing else to say.

At last he said, 'Is that what you came to tell me?' He looked at her in a different way now, and she was very conscious of the new brightness in his eyes.

She nodded. 'That was part of it.'

He smiled. 'You mean there's more?'

She stirred uncomfortably on the rock. 'I've had some long conversations with Aunt Cora.'

'About me?' he asked.

'Well, yes and no. Some were about you. About me. About the land. About other people.'

'What about the land?'

'I will inherit Aunt Cora's land someday.'

'There!' He jumped to his feet. 'Didn't I

know it!' he yelled. 'So that's why you came!' His face was thunderous. 'You are the conniving, mercenary American female I thought you to be! You came here to worm your way into that poor old lady's heart—and now you've done it! Shame on you! I thank my lucky stars I didn't allow myself to fall in love with you!'

Furious at his outburst, she jumped up. 'It's simply amazing how you can open your big mouth and Lydia Frazier LeDuke's words pour out! What are you—the LeDukes' ventriloquist's dummy?' She raked a hand through her hair impatiently. 'Thank your lucky stars you didn't fall in love with me! Ha! Before Lydia's finished with you, you'll most certainly wish you had fallen in love with me! You can count on that, my Lord Ashburton! But then it'll be too late! Like everything else in your life!'

'And what in the hell do you know about my life!'

Molly sank wearily back onto the rock. 'I know about you, Christopher. About your painting. About your injury. About Delilah.' She put her hand to her forehead. 'I *know* you.'

'Do you, now?' he said with a wry smile. 'Do you know me, Molly Rayner?'

A long silence.

Molly sighed. How could he misunderstand every word she ever spoke to him? She felt sorry, terribly sorry for them both. 'Why is it, Christopher, that it has been the hardest thing in the world for us merely to be friends? We undoubtedly love the same things in life, so why has it been so hard? So impossible for us?'

He studied her face.

'You're angry with me for looking at your portrait, when you shouldn't have been. You see, I know what face belongs there on that unpainted spot of canvas: the face you wore that day you first brought me here. An expression of pride. Of love.' She sat calmly, feeling small and tired. 'I'm keeping you from your fishing trip.'

He stared at her intently. 'You can still come with me,' he said awkwardly. 'If—if you'd like.'

'No.' She felt terribly tired. She shook her head and turned her back to him, starting to walk away. She felt the heat of his body behind her.

'Molly,' he said thickly. 'Please don't go.' His hands caught her shoulders and pulled her backward, close against the hardness of his body. 'From the first moment I saw you, I've felt I had to fight with you. If I ever stopped, I'd realize how much I loved you. I do, you know.' His lips brushed her ear passionately. 'I need you. I love you, Molly.'

Closing her eyes, she felt dizzy as his warm lips touched her neck, and his body pressed against hers. She felt his hand, gentle on her back, stroking her arms. His lips moved to her cheek.

'Kiss me. Kiss me, Molly,' he whispered. 'For once, kiss me.'

She moaned and twisted around in his arms. His lips crushed down on hers, silencing whatever words she was about to utter. Her arms slid around his neck, and she pressed herself against him.

'Oh, Christopher,' she murmured, pulling away, reluctantly forcing him to release her. 'You do love me.'

'Yes, I do. And I have for some time.' He touched her mouth gently with his fingertips. 'From the first moment I met you, to be exact.'

Her eyes widened. 'But—but what are we going to do?'

He smiled. 'The first thing we're going to do is go fishing. You must learn I'll not be outdone. I've spent all afternoon readying this old hull of a boat, and we're going to catch a fish. We'll fish and decide what to do.' Suddenly he laughed. 'At least you'll be safe in the boat, my darling. If we stay here, I couldn't promise you that.' He smiled at her, knowing she was onto his thin-skinned virtue. 'Come on, Molly, please go with me.'

Molly nodded. She had now gained what she had hoped for with all her heart. She

160

had learned that Christopher loved her. She would never be sorry for the torment she had gone through to learn it. His rage, his fear, his anger, had not ever been truly aimed against her—but against himself. Reaching the boat, she climbed in slowly.

Christopher's hand wrapped around her arm and she could feel his trembling. His lips again touched her neck, and she experienced a shock of pleasure at his touch.

She sat down, holding to the sides of the boat with both hands. 'How long will we be gone?'

He looked up at the sky. The dazzling red sun hovered close to the horizon of waves. 'Not over an hour. We'll tie in before dark. I promise. The wind is right, the tide is right, everything is right.' Untying the line, he threw it into the front of the boat, pushed the boat into the water, and leaped in. Settling himself on the seat facing her, he smiled and picked up the oars. 'I am so glad to have this out in the open. You can't imagine the nights I've lain awake and thought of you.'

She watched his arms, his strength, as he worked hard at the oars, taking them from the cove out to sea. 'Did you really, Christopher?' She sighed, relaxing. 'Did you really think about me? I thought only girls did foolish things like that.'

He was silent several long moments. 'Women don't always hold the monopoly on foolishness; some men are very foolish.' He winked at her.

Seabirds encircled the boat. The first red flush of sunset drifted across the quiet water. As soon as they were several hundred yards from shore Christopher dropped anchor and pulled the oars up into the oar-lock, reached into the bottom for his fishing gear, and a moment later cast his line into the water.

Molly would never forget that moment: the peaceful sea, the beautiful sky, and the wonderful warm feeling engulfing her. Indeed, of all precious moments in her life, this one was more precious than all others.

Christopher glanced over his shoulder at her. 'Do you want to fish?' he asked.

She shook her head. 'No, I'll just watch you.'

He grinned sheepishly. 'That could get boring.'

'I doubt it.' Elbows braced on knees, she propped her chin in her hands and watched him, her heart filled with wonder. No longer the sulking man she had met at the airport, no longer the arrogant brute who forever seemed to be grabbing her up in a kiss.

He reached down beside the boat and straightened his line. 'You know, I remember telling you that I loved you.' He cocked his head. 'But I don't remember you telling me that you loved me. Did you tell me?'

'I love you, Christopher,' she said, her voice low, yet filled with sureness. 'Very much,' she added. 'I love you.'

'Then why have you allowed me to dwell in such misery? I thought you detested the sight of me. Why have you done that, Molly?'

'Why have I done that?' she echoed, her eyes widening, her voice growing stronger. 'You—you say you love me, then why did you treat me like a stepsister? An unwanted one, at that!'

'Molly'—he looked impatient—'how can you accuse me of such things? It was you who rejected my advances.'

'Your advances? Me?' She stared at him; his face was aglow in the fading sunlight. 'Those weren't advances, Christopher. Those kisses were like warplanes attacking!'

'I had to kiss you that way. If I had kissed you in a calm, mannerly way, you would not have allowed me to kiss you at all.' The sun cast dancing flames in the green eyes. 'You despised me, Molly. I wanted you, and I wanted you to want me. All I ever saw in those blue American eyes was a total look of indifference. Admit it; it's true.'

'Ah, but Christopher, that's not true.' Her eyes scanned his face. 'One of us is going to have to begin to look more closely—the one of us who can't detect indifference from love.'

He laughed. 'You—you loved me, then?'

'Yes.' She inhaled deeply. 'But you weren't easy to love. What about that date you arranged with Russell?'

'I damn well deserve a flogging for that,' he agreed. 'I did it because I wanted you there at the dance with me, even though my evening was to be spent with'—he sighed—'Lydia.'

Molly straightened, clearing her throat. 'Incidentally, Lydia came to see me today.'

The light in his eyes vanished. 'Why?'

'To tell me to stay away from you; that the two of you are to soon be married.'

'That hardheaded wench! I've tried to tell her in a nice way that I don't love her, that I have no intentions of marrying her.'

'Apparently she doesn't understand. She was very adamant with her instructions.'

'I'll bet she was!' He breathed heavy with disgust. 'I tried to explain to her that I never loved her. What I thought was love was merely infatuation, and even that has vanished.'

The gentle wind off the water swept Molly's hair from her brow. The day grew cooler as the sun slid slowly behind the horizon.

'She would marry you anyway, even

164

knowing that you don't love her. Yes, she would still marry you.'

'No, that she will not do. Bigamy is illegal on these islands, I have selected the girl I intend to marry, and needless to say, that girl is not Lydia.'

'You've got a bite!' Molly yelled excitedly.

'Yes,' Christopher shouted. 'And he's a big one.' The fish ran out his line, then struggled; the bow of the boat sat down in the water. 'My God, he's a whale!' Christopher shouted. 'I'll never get him in.' He reached into the tackle box and removed a knife. Quickly he severed the line. The boat reeled and rocked, then finally leveled off.

'That was almost frightening.' Molly cleared her throat. 'I thought we were going to capsize.'

'That's what you call catching a fish too big to handle.' Turning, he looked up at the sky. 'I'd better take us in. It'll be dark before long, and I don't want you out on these roads after dark in that old truck.' He pulled up anchor and again his hands were on the oars.

She touched the backs of his hands lightly with the tips of her fingers as the oars came forward. A broad smile covered her face.

He glanced up at her, then he too smiled.

She really couldn't say what she felt. It was all too new. Unexpected and wonderfully new.

It seemed different to Christopher. The harder he rowed, the more he talked. 'The wind is rising. If we had a sail, we could fly back to shore. I love you, Molly.' He paused. 'Do you suppose Cora will be surprised?'

'I don't know, Christopher,' Molly said thoughtfully. 'Maybe a little surprised, but not *too* very surprised.'

Christopher chuckled. 'She's probably known all along. She did try to invent reasons for us to be together. I know that for a fact.'

Molly laughed. 'I'm sure she did.' She watched his arms and hands with the oars.

'My wrist is healed,' he said, watching her expression. 'That's why I went to England. I had a partial wrist replacement, an operation where the surgeon removed these two bones'—he pointed to his wrist—'and replaced them with a man-made joint. A ghastly-looking sort of contraption when it is outside the skin, but once inside it's quite beautiful.'

'You will paint again?'

'Oh, yes.'

'Will you finish your portrait?'

Releasing his grip on one oar, he reached out and clasped her hand. 'I promise to make amends for my behavior, and I will present the portrait with face to you as a

166

wedding present, to serve as a constant reminder to you what a perfect ass I can be.' He sighed. 'I promise.' He squeezed her hand gently.

The waves rippled quietly as he brought the boat to shore. Nothing outward had changed in the world. Yet Molly's entire inner world had become filled with such beauty she could lose her breath. The dream she had dared to dream had come true.

★   ★   ★

By midnight Molly still could not close her eyes. She wondered about the days ahead, her days with Christopher. She considered herself to be the luckiest girl on earth. She had met a man of worldly means, yet a man whose interest lay in the beauty of the world. In due time, she told herself with a smile, they would marry, raise a family on this island, but most of all, with his arms around her, she would be happy for the rest of her life. 'I, too, have seen your rainbow, Aunt Cora,' she murmured. 'And it is something wonderful to behold. Now, I can't wait for tomorrow!'

CHAPTER TWELVE

'You certainly must have things on your mind, dear,' Cora conceded with a smile. 'I'm sure it's none of my business, but old women are given to their periods of nosiness.'

'Yes,' Molly laughed, laying her head back against the sofa. 'It's wonderful! Absolutely wonderful!' She lay still, her sparkling eyes sweeping the ceiling. 'Christopher loves me! He wants to marry me,' she said, her voice filled with happiness. 'I'm going to spend the rest of my life with him, Aunt Cora.'

'I'm proud for both of you, dear,' Cora remarked, smiling. 'I have always considered Chris to be a very genuine sort of person; a little unsure of himself and his ambitions in life, but nevertheless, very genuine.'

Molly sat upright. Slender and fair, she wore a full skirt in a deep-rose shade and a crisp white blouse; her small feet were encased in delicate straps of black suede.

'Are you sure you want to drive into Auckland by yourself?' Cora asked, fussing around with a crocheted doily under the lamp. 'I'd be glad to go with you if it wasn't for my arthritis acting up.' She flinched her shoulders and straightened her arm. 'There's going to be a change in the weather; I feel it in my old bones.'

'I'll tell you what,' Molly said, grinning. 'You don't worry about me being in Auckland by myself today and I'll bring you back a doily that will fit right under that lamp.'

Molly was so happy she thought her heart would burst. Still she knew she had to occupy her mind this particular day. Despite her love for the ranch, she had to get away. The hours spent in the pastures with Sam and Jonathan passed too slowly. Feeling perfectly wonderful, she found an excuse to indulge herself—shopping in Auckland, spending the remainder of her life's savings on a wardrobe for the day she was to become Mrs. Christopher Ashburton. She wanted everything to be new and beautiful for him. With much enthusiasm she moved across the room in quick, light steps.

'I'll be back by midafternoon, Aunt Cora.'

'Watch the weather, dear,' Cora returned with maternal concern. 'It's going to do something out there today.'

The weather was the least of Molly's concerns. She knew Christopher would be seeing Lydia, and she was still dreadfully jealous of the black-haired model. Lydia was a conniver, and Molly knew she would not let go without a struggle. The LeDukes possessed nerves of steel.

With hours to kill before she saw Christopher in the evening, Molly drove slowly and carefully along the winding roads. A mile or so later, in the curve of the narrow farm road, she passed a car speeding in the direction of the Newcomb house.

She drove on a few yards, then threw on the brakes. In afterthought she realized the driver of that car was Russell LeDuke. Obviously he must have recognized her, for in the rearview mirror she saw the taillights backing toward her. Oh, no! What does he want? Molly wondered apprehensively. Fighting an overwhelming temptation to drive on as he walked toward her, she sat awkwardly until he knocked on her window with his knuckles.

Frowning, she lowered the glass. 'Hello, Russell. What's up?'

'Where are you off to on this fine day?' he asked lightly.

'That is none of your business,' she returned rudely, noticeably eager to be rid of him.

'You're mistaken there, Molly,' he said with a glint in his eyes. 'I'm here on business. Important business, for a fact.' Moving slowly, he opened her car door, caught her slender waist firmly, and pulled. 'Come on out,' he said, his voice low, cunning. 'This might take a while.'

'Take your hands off me!' she snapped rebelliously, snatching her arm from his grip.

'Whatever you say,' he mused. 'But I'll not talk to you while you're in that car.'

'I'm not getting out,' she said determinedly. 'Besides, I'm not interested in any more of your lies!'

His angry eyes flew wide open. Then he laughed sardonically. 'I would say we're at a stalemate, but that's to your disadvantage, Molly darling. For what I have to say concerns your happiness—and Christopher's!'

Her face paled. In spite of her anger, she slowly opened the door wide and stepped onto the road. After pushing the door closed, she raised furious eyebrows at him. 'Speak.'

He turned indifferently and walked a few steps. 'I'm not a dog,' he muttered with cruel irony. 'Don't ever order me in that tone of voice again.'

'What do you want, Russell?' she cried out, thoroughly exasperated. 'I am out of the car!' She realized she was playing right into his hands, but she was at the point where she couldn't leave. Up until he mentioned Christopher's name, she could have; but when Russell did that, she helplessly became his pawn in this game of words. To her dismay, he wasn't yet ready to divulge what was lurking in his mind.

'Let's go somewhere comfortable,' he said. 'Let's sit under that tree.' He pointed to a large oak a few feet from the road.

With a dismal sigh, she followed. As she left the road her high heel pivoted on a rock, and she stumbled, painfully twisting her ankle. She grimaced, holding inward a sharp cry. Managing to hobble the next few feet, she lowered herself into a sitting position near the gigantic trunk. She leaned back and straightened her leg, carefully trying to work her ankle, which had already begun to swell. She cringed in pain.

'Is it broken?' he asked, his voice distinctly cool.

Confusion in her mind, pain radiating up her leg, she screamed out, 'Don't ask about my ankle—just tell me!' The strain of the moment showed clearly on her face.

Playing for time, enjoying himself immensely, Russell bent down and grabbed her leg. 'I was a boy scout,' he said, pressing his fingers into the swollen ankle. 'Bet you didn't know that. Wait here,' he commanded, rising to his feet. 'I've got something in the car that will serve as a bandage.'

Tears welled up. 'I don't want a bandage. I don't give a damn that you were a boy scout! Just tell me!'

172

'I'm not saying anything until I bandage that ankle.'

She felt like exploding. Her sprained ankle had given him added time—added time to drag out this crazy game. She watched him go to his car and remove a first-aid kit from the glove compartment; then he reached down and picked something up from the front seat. Halfway back, she recognized it: a newspaper. Carefully folded and tucked neatly under his arm.

Squatting at her feet, he frowned. 'Looks real bad. It could be broken.'

She clenched her hands in anger. 'Please hurry, Russell.' She spoke with much more control than she felt. 'I'm in a bit of a rush.'

'After I finish, we'll talk. Now be a good girl and hold still.' Suddenly his mouth tightened with anger, his brown eyes darkened. He continued to wrap her ankle, the paper tucked away close to his armpit. 'There,' he said, dropping her foot onto the ground. 'It's done.' He stood, towering over her.

With exasperating composure she said, 'Can we get on with it?' She eyed the newspaper.

'Of course.' He smiled. 'Let's do get on with it. First, let's discuss our forthcoming marriage—yours and mine!'

'You're insane!' Outraged, flushing red,

173

Molly jumped to her feet. For a split second she forgot about her ankle. 'Oh!' she screamed, her arms swinging wildly through the air. Losing her balance, she fell to her knees.

Immediately he knelt beside her. 'Look what you've done! Now, it's probably broken for sure!'

She didn't seem to hear. Closing her eyes, she leaned her head back against the tree. She was alone with a madman. Russell LeDuke had to be completely and totally mad. 'Oh, Christopher,' she cried out in her mind, 'please help me.'

'Open your eyes and look at me, Molly,' he ordered. 'I know you think I'm crazy, but let me assure you, I'm not! Open your eyes and look at me!'

She glanced at him apprehensively from the corner of her eye. A frightful tremor swept through her. Her breathing was rapid; her ankle stung as if attacked by a bed of ants.

His eyes traveled over her fleetingly. 'Does the thought of marrying me chill your blood, my darling?' he asked smoothly.

'Marrying you waits some distance behind the very last thing I will do on this earth.'

'Now, now, don't say something that you might regret later. I'm really not a beast, Molly. And now that Christopher's out of the picture...'

'How dare you—' she began.

Not intending for her to finish, he cut in, 'It's nothing personal, Molly. You must understand this from the outset. I'm not deriving any real pleasure from this.'

'I'll just bet you're not!' she replied, amazed at his gall.

'It's just that Christopher should be more careful about his engagements.'

'Engagements?' She stared at him, startled.

'That's correct. Engagements,' he assured her.

She felt the heat rushing throughout her entire body.

'I'm speaking now as Lydia's brother. Christopher asked for her hand in marriage and she accepted his proposal.'

'So?' Molly whispered, bitterness escaping in her words. 'That was Christopher's mistake. He realizes it and is taking steps to correct it.'

'Yes, it was a mistake, but you just don't go around breaking engagements— particularly to the governor's daughter.'

'Christopher will.' She lifted her head and stared head-on at him. She could imagine Christopher standing in the governor's mansion, refusing to be intimidated by the LeDuke clan. She knew his temper, the height of his emotions, as perhaps no one else did. His jawline and mouth when set in

175

anger, the raised brows signifying dangerous emotions.

Russell's expression was a mixture of haughtiness and amusement. He ignored her bittersweet and impertinent reply: 'No, he did not break the engagement.'

A moment of fleeting despair winged through her. A look of disbelief filled her face.

'I suggest you listen to me now, for I'm speaking as an attorney of law, no longer the brother of the bride-to-be.'

Molly's eyes stormed with rebellion. 'I don't care what you speak as, I refuse to believe anything you say. I know what Christopher can and cannot do. I know a man cannot be forced into marrying a woman he doesn't love!'

Russell studied her with a degree of speculation. 'I'm going to be patient with you, Molly, unless you push me too far.'

Their eyes clashed, his dark ones mocking hers.

'Now, everyone knows of Lydia's engagement to Christopher. Everyone in this dominion knows. It's what you call common knowledge. For all intents and purposes an engagement such as this is equal to marriage.' Amusement again played in his voice. 'You might even say the marriage has been consummated, even though the vows have not officially been spoken. You do know Lydia has stayed at his home overnight on many occasions?' He grinned broadly. 'The two of them have been very close—very close indeed.'

Closing her eyes, Molly tried to ignore his biting words. He was hammering away at her for a purpose, trying to break her down. He'll never do it, Christopher, she vowed silently. I'll never let him do it.

'I'm just looking out for what is rightfully Lydia's,' he said. 'I agree some of her actions have been foolish, but they were foolish enough to seal Christopher into a contract he can't break.'

The entire matter was taking a strange shape. 'You're lying! I know you're lying! In spite of whatever unconventional action has transpired between Christopher and Lydia, he cannot be forced into marrying her!'

He laughed at her open countenance. 'My, my, you sound like an attorney yourself, Molly. I didn't realize you were so knowledgeable in the aspects of law.'

She ignored him as if he had not spoken. 'I wouldn't put anything past you, Russell. You'd stoop to anything—and apparently Lydia would too—to get your greedy hands on this land. I know what you're up to.'

'Do you? Do you really?'

'I seem to recall a bunch of lies,' she retorted. 'If only I'd stopped to think at the time, I would have realized you were telling lies. Christopher loves this land, but he doesn't want Aunt Cora's, at least not enough to lie and connive to get it! I know that's where the difference is; you and Lydia will do anything to place your grubby little hands on it, and I know why! Money! Greed! If you had it there wouldn't be any stock here then. No forest. No clean beaches. There'd only be oil wells pumping that black gold into your pockets!'

Her outburst left him unmoved. 'You're quite wrong!' he said, not moving a muscle. 'But either way, right or wrong, it's beside the point. Lydia is Christopher's fiancée, and she *will* become his wife. The sooner you adjust yourself to that fact, the better off you will be.'

Her eyebrows flicked up. 'I will never adjust to that fact!' she cried, outraged by his arrogance. 'I, not Lydia, will marry Christopher! Wait and see!'

Russell LeDuke was way beyond anything she had ever seen. She stared at him with disbelief. No matter what he said or threatened, never, never would she believe him.

'Look.' He removed the paper from under his arm. In a quick movement he jerked it open and forced it in her face. 'Look at the front page! Not in the social section where formal engagements are usually announced–but the front page!'

She stared at the headline of the *Auckland Post* for a long, long moment. Lydia LeDuke's black-and-white picture smiled demurely at her. The headlines blared out:

GOVERNOR'S DAUGHTER
TO MARRY NOBLEMAN

A cold twinge of fear began in the base of her soul.

Russell dropped the paper and grabbed her shoulders roughly. 'Perhaps now my story has a bit more credibility. Huh? Do you believe me now, Molly?'

Totally distraught, she glared at him. It could not be true. Christopher would make it right. Of course, how silly of me, the paper was printed before Christopher had a chance to break off with Lydia. Now she understood Russell's game.

'And to think that dumb, big-boned jackass came to the house today to tell her it was off!' He laughed gleefully, the game nearly ended. 'Can you believe that! He asked Lydia to forgive him, but it seemed he didn't love her after all. I must admit he didn't use much discretion, waiting until the papers were full of the news.'

Her mind whirled. She could not move her astounded eyes from his face.

'That is, he didn't love her until he realized what was at stake. Then I quickly informed him that if he proceeded to embarrass Lydia with publicity of a broken

179

engagement to marry some waif of an American nobody, I would file a breach-of-promise action on her behalf that would literally clean him of all earthly possessions. His land here and in England. I could get everything he owns for Lydia through the courts of law.' His hands tightened. 'There *will* be a wedding.'

Russell was holding her shoulders exactly where Christopher had held them only yesterday. She felt she would surely explode beneath the building pressures. 'Don't touch me, Russell,' she said calmly. 'Not now—or ever again!'

'Sure, my dear.' He smiled, relaxing his grip, then removed his hands completely.

She gazed into his face. 'Get out of my sight,' she whispered.

'Sure. Sure.' He laughed nervously. 'But I'll be seeing you again. You can count on that!'

Motionless, her face stony, she watched him walk confidently to his car and drive away.

CHAPTER THIRTEEN

Catching a fish too big to handle. That's what he'd done when he caught Lydia Frazier LeDuke. Molly looked around. The sweet smell of New Zealand was everywhere. She felt nothing. Absolutely nothing.

She leaned back against the oak and closed her eyes. In her mind she saw the red-tinted waves of the sea as it had looked last night. Last night with Christopher. The calm, tranquil sea. His warm lips kissing her. All her thoughts were running together. In her mind the sea wasn't tranquil any longer, but raging waves swept across, drowning, drowning her dreams.

Slowly she pulled herself up and hobbled back to the truck. Christopher wouldn't come. With those eyes so clear and green—he would not be able to face her with them.

She knew that Russell was a magnificent liar, yet she also knew he wasn't lying this time. The *Auckland Post* verified his story. Christopher had walked into the LeDukes' lion's den just as he had promised.

She leaned forward, her breasts resting against the steering wheel; she cringed from the pain radiating up her left leg. She turned the key. The full impact finally hit. 'Oh, Christopher,' she cried aloud. 'I love you! Is this really happening? What will happen to us now? If you marry Lydia, what will that make me? Will you still love me? Even when you're married to her, will you still love me?'

181

In terrible pain, physically and emotionally exhausted, she backed the car and turned around in the road. There was no answer to any of the tormenting questions. She drove wildly, the car wheels screeching along the road, the sudden onslaught of tears half blinding her.

She wouldn't be going to Auckland now. Her savings would not be spent on a wedding wardrobe. No indeed; the LeDukes had seen to that.

The memory of snuggling against Christopher's chest last night, the memory of his eyes smiling tenderly at her—it had been real. Why didn't we run away last night, Christopher? Why didn't we just run away? Now it's too late. She studied the land bordering the road. Lonely, hard, beautiful wild land—land she had grown to love.

Suddenly the car made a peculiar tremor, a sideways swaying movement in the road. 'Don't you play out on me, you crazy old car,' she said, grasping the wheel tighter.

There must be something I can do, she thought. Something to ease this terrible, terrible pain in my heart. She felt a sudden desire to laugh; but pressing her fist against her lips, she would not allow the hollow sounds to escape. Instinctively she knew that to laugh now would perhaps take her out of touch with reality. Enough tears would eventually fill the void in her made by fleeing emotions. Tears were real and could be weighed, but laughter was hollow and could only pass through the void, leaving it untouched.

Seeing the house in the distance, she pressed the brake. She drew in a long breath and looked at the sprawling white structure she now called home. 'Run, Molly,' a voice taunted her. 'Run. Run while you can.' She looked past the house to the stable. Delilah.

Her eyes widened. She hesitated a moment longer, then without thought or direction, she released the brake and pressed hard on the accelerator. She sped past the house, the garage, and screeched to an abrupt halt at the fence gate. She wiped the dampness from her forehead with the back of her hand. She felt strange, as though her tight chest was forcibly being stretched with each breath she drew. For a moment she thought she felt a strangeness, an incredible crushing of the atmosphere.

Slinging the gear into park, she brought the truck to a halt, then climbed out and limped to the gate. Opening it, she hobbled inside. The sleek black mare stood a few feet away, eyeing Molly's every movement.

'Delilah,' Molly called out softly, urgently. 'Come here, girl. Come here.'

Delilah moved towards her as if she understood what Molly was feeling.

Kicking off her shoes, impatient with the pain in her ankle, Molly stood in her stocking feet. 'Come here, girl,' she said again. With supreme control of her painful movements, she went into the stable and returned lugging a saddle and bridle. 'Let's you and I go for one last ride,' she whispered.

Delilah stood poised with such strength that Molly felt a small degree of comfort—the first since seeing Russell. She spoke to the mare all the time she worked, trying to cover all outward signs of emotion. She felt the remaining color drain from her cheeks as she pulled herself up into the saddle. She must not think of pain. Not physical nor emotional. In absolute freeness she and Delilah would travel the land from the south boundary to the north, from the coastline to the mountains. It would be her last glimpse of the island. Tomorrow she would return to America.

One hand on the rein, she leaned over and unlatched the gate, and Delilah high-stepped through the opening.

'Molly!'

Molly turned her attention to the house. Aunt Cora had come running out the back door.

'Molly!' Alarmed, she called out again, 'Molly, wait!'

'Don't worry, Aunt Cora, we'll be back.'

'Wait! Wait, Molly!'

With her right stocking foot Molly nudged Delilah. The mare gave a quick jerk, then threw back her proud head and galloped at high speed past the fenced pasture and up, then down, the hillside. For a moment Molly forgot all else but the dry wind whistling past her ears, striking her face with a vengeance. No longer thinking—she was feeling. Through her feelings she was beginning to understand the truth.

The LeDukes had raised an insurmountable barrier between her and Christopher: the LeDuke world of power. Getting, taking, accomplishing, conniving, struggling to extend their power to the greatest possible measure. Whatever the cost. To think, her day of happiness had scarcely begun when Russell LeDuke ended it. She felt so helpless, yet there was nothing to do but nudge Delilah faster. Faster until the wind in her face obliterated all thoughts in her mind. The horizon became lost to her, blurred into an unrecognizable haze.

Finally Delilah slowed into a brisk trot along the beach, her hooves resounding loud on the hard sand. 'Okay, girl,' Molly whispered, rubbing the mare's neck. 'We'll slow down awhile. I know you're tired.'

Molly raised her eyes and looked out across the sea. The water looked different:

dark, cold, uninviting. Pulling Delilah to a halt, she dismounted gingerly. Holding the rein, she led Delilah to a dune at the west edge of the beach, away from the water. She sat down, kicking a piece of driftwood with her good foot. She looked up and down the stretch of sand; not a sign of life anywhere. Not even a sea gull. The hushed waves seemed to gurgle a strange noise as they lapped against the packed sand.

How could the part of her life with Christopher be over? It had not even begun. She thought about Russell, feeling nothing but extreme disgust for him. What did he think? What prompted him? Did he believe that once Lydia and Christopher were married he could then come calling on her like nothing had happened? Was that what he thought? If it was, he had a surprise in store. Tears welled in her eyes, and she quickly swallowed and brushed them away.

The sea she had always thought of as so beautiful looked strange—in a way she couldn't identify. The waves seemed harsh and unfriendly as they battered away at the sand. She bent down and picked up a small seashell, then threw it swirling through space onto the beach. It bounced into the water and disappeared.

That's what it was. The water was dark, not clear and bubbly as usual. Turning her eyes upward, she scanned the sky. Suddenly she felt a dampness, a coolness, and wondered if the gray clouds moving in from the horizon would bring rain. It didn't matter. Rain wouldn't hurt her. The rose skirt and white blouse were already stained and splattered with dust. She looked down at her toes protruding from the end of her hose; there were wide runs in her nylons. She leaned over and pressed her fingers into her ankle. She winced in pain. Nevertheless, she slowly unwrapped the bandage Russell had placed around it, wadded it into a ball, and threw it at the water.

She watched the big surf for a moment, then rose and aimlessly led Delilah along the beach. She felt shaken and helpless and her ankle pained her terribly.

Suddenly there came a grunt, a faraway sound; the earth seemed to sway beneath her feet for a moment. Lurching forward she scrambled to keep her balance.

Delilah balked, throwing her head wildly.

'Whoa, girl. Whoa.' She fought hard to keep Delilah from breaking free. Wrapping the reins around her hands she held on for dear life. Delilah finally quieted, twitched her hide nervously; big black eyes blinked at her rider.

Molly touched the mare's head gently. 'Now, girl, it's okay. That was just that big wave rolling in. Come on, let's you and me go check on the sheep.'

Astride the mare again, Molly looked back to the sea, took a deep breath, and turned Delilah inland. The world seemed very solemn—hushed and cool and dark—as the mare stepped high across the bush land leading to the pastures.

Absorbed in silence, Molly wondered if Christopher would finish his portrait. 'It's mine, Christopher,' she wanted to scream. 'You promised it to me.' In that bitter moment she wept, crying aloud into the tight atmosphere.

Now Christopher would never know her. They would never make love. She would never snuggle against him in the middle of the night. He would never see the sharp contrast of their skin—his, tanned and muscular; hers, frail and white against his. He would never see her in the silken folds of her négligee or watch the night shadows play across her body. He would never know with what depths she loved him—and would always love him.

The wet marks of tears glistened on her face, and in tired defeat she slumped in the saddle.

His warm and powerful body, exciting and filled with life; his smile; the vital passions lighting his green eyes; the ultimate thrill of belonging to him. 'Christopher. Christopher,' she groaned into the cool air. In a sudden, almost savage movement she brought her bare heels back against Delilah and slapped the reins against the mare's neck.

The shiny black mare took off in a flash across the hillside, appearing and vanishing over the rolling hills. Again she slowed on her own accord.

In the near distance Molly heard the bleat of sheep and the sound of Jonathan's dog barking. A thin mist hovered over the valley. She could not see the animals with their heavy coats of thick wool, but she heard them.

Pulling to a halt beside the makeshift shelter, Molly called out to Sam and Jonathan. No answer. She called again at the top of her voice. Still no answer.

Alighting from Delilah, she turned her loose to graze, then sat down on the grass, wondering where the ranch hands were at this time of day.

An eternity seemed to pass in those few seconds. The ground where she sat was hot, and for a moment she felt as though it were shaking. She found herself leaning to the right, off balance in a weird sort of way. She heard a bird in a tree nearby, not singing its usual song, but making an awful screeching noise.

Placing both hands flat on the ground, Molly steadied herself. She frowned. Probably the jolts she had experienced along with the strong wind slapping her head had caused a disturbance in her inner ear. That had happened to her once in Philadelphia. She had developed dizziness and loss of balance following a virus infection. There had been nothing to worry about; the disorder had cleared up in a few days. That was how she felt now. Dizzy and off balance.

She looked around at Delilah. The mare was not grazing. Rather, she stood very still, as if listening for something, the large eyes not blinking.

'You better eat, girl,' Molly said in little above a whisper. 'We'll have to be going home soon.' Propping her arms behind her head, Molly stretched out on the ground. The throb in her ankle became almost unbearable, and she had reached a point of near total exhaustion.

Closing her eyes, she found herself reliving her encounter with Christopher last night. She kept remembering the soft sureness of his voice, the tenderness in his eyes, when he had said, 'I love you, Molly. I love you.' How could he have told her then, with such sincerity, that he loved her, and today resume his marriage plans with Lydia Frazier? How could that be? One or the other couldn't be real. Which was it?

She bolted into a sitting position and pressed her palms to her forehead. She didn't know for sure that Christopher had given in to the LeDukes' demands. All she had was Russell's word. She clamped her lips together.

Russell's eyes had been narrow, challenging, daring her to believe him. His insinuation had been so overpowering. Somehow from the onset he had known she would eventually believe him. But he had considered it necessary to bring the paper, the *Auckland Post*, to verify his story. A final threat to her.

She clutched her head again. She didn't know what to believe. Tears of anger and frustration poured down her cheeks. Why had she run away before seeing if Christopher would come and tell her everything would be all right? Her self-pride, the humiliation of being caught up so helplessly in a situation, could not allow her to face the possibility that he would not come. That's why she had run. But what if he had come and Aunt Cora told him that she had run off on Delilah? Knowing how he felt about the mare, she realized he would know then that it was her love, and not his, that had weakened and crumbled beneath Russell's facade of lies.

She bit her lip hard. What a fool I've been!

She struggled to her feet. 'Let's go, Delilah,' she whispered. 'Let's go home.'

Delilah's ears pricked forward, but she made no attempt to move. Again her skin twitched nervously as Molly hoisted herself up into the saddle.

And again Molly heard the sudden panicked cry of the bird.

Unable to account for the eerie sensation traveling the length of her spine, Molly looked around. An uneasy stillness had settled on the earth. She sensed the growing tension in the mare. Not sure why, Molly felt the same tension growing in herself.

She listened. The sheep were running, bleating and clamoring to the far side of the pasture. The barking of Jonathan's dog had turned into an uncanny howl. From the kauri pine forest animals were running into the open, away from the towering trees.

What in God's name is happening! The mare reared and screamed a loud whinny. Molly held onto the reins with all her strength. 'Let's go, Delilah!' she pleaded in a soft whisper. 'Let's go. Please.'

The mare leaped forward and thrashed along the path leading from the pastures. Molly felt a strong vibration travel along her legs. 'Hurry! Hurry, Delilah!'

A hollow roar erupted from out of nowhere. It was a sound she'd heard before. But where? The beach? Yes, she'd heard the same sound earlier at the beach—but she was away from the sea now.

The sky darkened as if night had fallen suddenly, without warning. Climbing the hill, she looked over her shoulder. A tall pine seemed to jump from the ground, then reeled momentarily in midair and crashed forward.

Delilah leaped over a creek in a dead run. 'Hang on,' Molly told herself. 'Hang on!' Her eyes widened in disbelief as the stream abruptly changed its course under the mare's hooves.

The world was collapsing, coming apart before her very eyes. Earthquake.

The noises kept coming. Louder and closer.

Delilah's feet were pounding the earth as hard as they could go. Twice she lost her footing and stumbled, but hurriedly straightened and again pounded the surface faster ... faster. Heading for home.

Dazed, Molly clung to the reins with all her strength.

The tremors were coming only a few seconds apart now. Any moment she expected the earth to open up and swallow horse and rider.

A cold shudder ran through her body. She saw it coming. Refusing to believe it—still she saw it coming. Looking down she gasped.

A crack had cut the earth in two and was travelling a jagged path toward her.

In a split second the terrified Delilah stood on her hind legs, flailing the air with her front hooves.

Tumbling backward through the air, her mind reeling under the impact of what was happening, Molly had time for one thought. One word:

'Christopher!'

Then her world went black.

CHAPTER FOURTEEN

Molly heard only the faint sound of Jonathan's dog howling. The earth lay in absolute silence. For a moment she felt suspended in an atmosphere she could not comprehend. She held her breath, avoiding even the slightest movement. The pain in her ankle was like a streak of fire. Again she heard the sound of the dog howling and she shuddered.

With a pang she remembered the earth trembling violently, the ground opening up, the jagged crevice stretching deep before Delilah's hooves. The mare had bolted. Molly remembered seeing the front hooves frantically fighting the air. And then there was nothing. How long had she lain unconscious? She shivered, trying to move her body; every muscle seemed to work against her. It was as if life had stopped and she was trying to get it back again. She must...

Slowly opening her eyes, she raised her head. She regarded the sight around her in hopeless disbelief. Uprooted trees lay all around. Panicked, she pushed her left hand against the soil in an attempt to raise herself from the ground. The soil crumbled beneath her outstretched palm and went rolling down the crevice. She quickly rolled to her right and began to crawl away from the deep gorge. She pulled herself over a pile of stones and tumbled over, face up to the dark sky.

Frantically trying to grasp her bearings, she knew she was somewhere between the beach and the pastures. Completely isolated. She struggled to quell the rising scream originating from the depth of her soul. She had witnessed the earth bursting apart, had seen the trees come up, the soil clinging to their roots, plucked by a forceful power as if they were no more than bitterweeds. Supposing the ground had opened up beneath Aunt Cora's house? Supposing Christopher had been driving around in his Jeep? Christopher!

High above her head she heard a gull shrieking. Still the thudding of her heart seemed louder than the shrill cry of the gull. What would be waiting for her when she got home? Would she ever get home? The thought of Christopher and Aunt Cora brought a surge of strength to her. She rose to her knees, crawling from rock to rock, from jutting hillocks to grass-covered chunks of turf scattered along the route to the beach.

'I—I must get to the beach. There I will know where I am. I can get home.' Deliberately closing her mind to all else, she struggled, inching her way eastward. Heavy clouds were banking over all horizons. Pausing for breath, she looked up at the heavy gray and black streaks hovering low across the sky. She feared that there might be another quake, as unexpected, as devastating. Her heart stopped.

She thought again of Jonathan's dog. She had not heard it bark in a while. And Delilah? In helpless revulsion, she thought of the spirited mare being caught in one of the wide cracks in the earth.

Something caught her eyes. Emerging from behind a bush, she pulled herself down the rise toward the beach. The hard-packed white sand seemed undisturbed. She looked out across the surface of the water where swelling breakers thundered toward the shoreline. She listened. A strange gurgling, swirling sound erupted from the sea; it was an endless sound, an angry and unrelenting sound.

Confused and frightened, Molly laid her head across her arms, stretching out her aching body along the rise. She had no power to drag herself back. Her strength was spent. In a swift nervous movement she pushed back her hair and turned her head toward the ocean.

In a flash of comprehension she realized what was happening. The tide was coming, growing louder as it loomed up against the horizon. Her chest tightened. A hundred yards out in the sea she saw a tremendous wave rushing inland—a wave that would drown all the beach and anything else that happened to be in its path. Its crest seemed to reach up and touch the darkened sky.

A barely audible cry escaped her throat—a cry that vanished against the heightened roar. It was nearly there; she felt the earth trembling beneath her. There seemed to be nothing to do, nowhere to go. She held back the despairing cry that rose to her lips.

In a fleeting second she thought of Christopher and Aunt Cora. In a misery of half-consciousness, the thought of them roused her. Some strong instinct for survival propelled her to her feet. The pain of her swollen ankle cutting into her like a knife, she ran inland, not looking back.

There seemed to be no sound on earth except the deafening roar. Impatiently brushing a hand across her eyes, she wiped away the tears, which threatened to obscure her vision. She ran along the narrow winding path that led up to the hillside and the grazing pastures. The cold salty water lapped at her heels. She ran faster, feeling very, very helpless. With one last surge of willpower she ran up the hillside, her breath coming in short, heaving gasps. She had done all she could do.

Closing her eyes to the gray world, she sank to her knees; her muscles quivered uncontrollably and a peaceful oblivion began to descend.

As if in slow motion, she fell onto the grass. Her eyes closed, and she hovered somewhere between two worlds. She could see Christopher's face; it seemed to be bending close to her own, yet she knew it was merely a dream, for her eyelids were weighted closed.

Then it was no longer Christopher's face, gentle, worried, concern etched in the lines beside his eyes. No, it was not the face of the man she loved. Distorted and evil, the face thrusting itself upon her mind belonged to Russell LeDuke. The face came closer, smirking and taunting her.

She lay there in a dead sleep.

★　　　★　　　★

Her limbs felt numb and paralyzed when at last she stirred. One nightmare had ended. And she was alive.

Hearing voices in the distance, she realized that people were nearby. She could hear them yelling out to one another. Jonathan ... Sam ... fussing and grumbling back and forth. She tried to open her eyes but didn't have the strength to stir.

Another voice sounded: 'Here she is! I've found her!'

There was no mistaking that voice. A moment later she felt herself caught up in his arms. Wonderful, warm arms; arms that pulled her close to his powerful body.

'She's unconscious. Quick, Sam, bring the Jeep!' An urgency in his voice. She felt his face in her hair; heard him whisper, 'Thank God. Thank God.'

She could feel the wonderful tranquil sensation of his arms holding her close. Everything was all right.

'You drive, Jonathan,' he ordered. 'Sam, help me! Hurry!'

She wanted to tell Christopher she was all right, to reach up and touch his face. She wanted to see him smile down at her. She tried to move her lips, lift her hand, but it was as if her muscles had been severed from her brain's control. She knew his arms were around her; she could feel them. She could feel her head against his shoulder, and his shirt damp with perspiration. She could feel the Jeep speeding hurriedly down the road, the wheels bouncing over rocks and striking holes.

Sam shouted something to Jonathan, something about getting them all killed, but the old warrior's voice was no match for the loud roar of the motor. She felt Christopher's arms tighten around her, and a heavy void of black sleep came toward her. She fought it, but in a split second she lost the battle and felt herself succumb to the sweeping blackness.

★　　　★　　　★

When she opened her eyes, she found herself in a place she had not been in before. The walls were a bland green tile. A light shone in her face; a tiny light came toward her eyes, which blurred everything. Then the small light disappeared. Through the haze she saw Aunt Cora and, beside her, Christopher. They were talking to a man wearing a long white coat.

She reached out to them.

Cora Newcomb, seeing the movement, ran over to the bed. She clasped Molly's hand in her own. 'Dear,' she whispered, on the verge of tears. 'Can you hear me?'

Molly nodded very slightly.

'You took a bad fall. The doctor says you

have a concussion, but you'll be okay in a few days. Your ankle is badly sprained but not broken.' She went on talking: 'We were so worried about you. After the quake, when Delilah came home without you, we feared the worst.'

Molly moistened her parched lips. 'Delilah?' she whispered faintly.

'Oh, yes, Delilah's home. At this moment she's in the stall eating oats as though nothing at all had happened.'

Molly closed her eyes. She was alive. She would get well. Then she felt a strong hand stroking her fingers lightly.

'Rest now,' he said softly. 'We'll be able to take you home in a day or so.'

She wasn't worried anymore. He loved her. He had said 'We'll . . . take you home in a day or so.' Not Cora will take you home, but we will.

Suddenly she knew she had to tell him what had happened. Tell him why she had run away on Delilah. He had to know; he had to know about Russell.

Again she opened her eyes.

Green ones were smiling down at her tenderly.

She swallowed hard. 'Russell . . .' She gasped weakly. 'Russell . . .' But she could not finish.

She saw a strained expression flood his face. Suddenly his features hardened as if set in stone. He blinked down at her, wide-eyed in disbelief.

His hand disappeared from hers. With a sudden hard composure he turned to Cora. 'I see I'm not needed here, Cora,' he said stiffly. 'I'll wait for you in the car.'

Tears of frustration built up behind Molly's eyes, but crying took strength and she couldn't muster enough to shed a single tear. Great racking sobs tore her apart inwardly.

CHAPTER FIFTEEN

Molly sat huddled beside the living room window, looking out at the gardens, breathing in the fresh scents of the tropical flowers, and watching a tiny tui bird jump from bush to bush in search of a place suitable for his song. The sun-fired sky was dazzling blue, and she saw only an occasional puff of cloud float by. Curling up against the pillow in her chair, Molly thought how curious is the earth. Deliberately cruel and full of destruction one day; brilliantly clear and full of life the next.

'Molly, darling, can I get anything for you?' Cora came into the room, her voice filled with devotion to her blue-eyed niece.

'Are you comfortable?'

Molly replied with a quick 'No, thank you, Aunt Cora. Yes, I'm comfortable.' She didn't enjoy being a helpless patient. Her headache had finally left, and she could take a few steps on her foot without it giving way under her.

'Christopher is coming for tea,' Cora stated nonchalantly as she dusted a spot from the coffee table with a corner of her apron.

Molly stirred in the chair, her heart suddenly beating fast with apprehension. 'Why is he doing that?'

Cora straightened her apron. 'He likes my tea, I suppose,' she said with a very light trace of mirthfulness. 'Of course, he and I have had some business transactions these past few days that will need finalizing.'

'I'm sure he will not want me present then.' Molly kept her eyes on the outside world, the world beyond the window.

Cora cleared her throat. 'I was under the impression that you were in love with him, Molly. Was I mistaken?'

'No.' Molly swallowed hard. 'But apparently he doesn't believe it. You saw how he acted at the hospital when I tried to tell him about Russell.'

'No, dear, I heard you call Russell's name—twice, to be exact. Just what Christopher heard.'

'But I was trying to explain to him what had happened!'

'Christopher didn't realize that was what you were trying to do.' A smile curved on her lips. 'If he had, I'm sure he wouldn't have left in such a state. An Englishman in love is a strange creature indeed. You wounded his pride. I have never witnessed such anguish on anyone's face.'

'Aunt Cora,' Molly said almost fiercely. 'I was only trying to explain!'

'I know, Molly.' Cora sighed. 'But, dear, I wish you had waited until you could have said the complete sentence strong and loud: "Russell LeDuke is a lowdown snake in the grass!" Then Christopher would not have had to suffer because you called the slimy creature's name. Do you understand what I am saying?' She raised her eyebrows.

'Oh, yes, I understand! But do you understand'—her eyes clouded—'how hurt I was when he stormed out of that room? Can you possibly know how that hurt me?'

'I'm sure that both of you have had your emotions thoroughly wrung out by this LeDuke deal. But I am equally sure that you'll both survive and probably be happier someday because of it.'

'How can you say that?' Startled, Molly raised her voice.

Cora Newcomb smiled angelically. 'Because I am an old woman, dear, and old

204

women can say anything they please.' She strolled out of the room, humming a little tune under her breath.

Molly could feel her heart hammering away in her chest as she looked out the window. Even if Christopher knew the reason behind her speaking Russell's name in her semiconscious state, the basic problem was still there. The LeDukes were not people to make hollow threats. She longed for Christopher to get there and tell her what was to happen to them. How wonderful it would be to slip into his arms and hear him say everything would be all right. What a burden it would lift from her weary mind.

The earthquake did not change the facts. Her mind wandered unceasingly. The major damage had occurred to the land; the sheep were safe, the house was unharmed, and no one outside of herself had suffered injury—and her greatest injury had occurred long before the earth tremored.

How could she expect Christopher to face a court battle with the LeDukes for her sake? Even if he loved her—and she knew he did—how could she expect his love for her to be greater than his love for his beautiful estate and all his possessions? His face was not a mask to her. She had witnessed his expression the day he drove her to his home. Her heart understood his feelings. How could people like the LeDukes be so cruel in their vain ambitions that they could distort the dreams of others and shatter lives because of greed.

Preoccupied with her thoughts, she did not see or hear the car until it stopped in front of the house. A strange feeling swept across her as she watched him step from the automobile and look toward the house. With a quick movement she shied away from the window. Seeing him, she wished she had dressed differently; she knew the cream-colored cotton dress did not flatter her pale cheeks but added to the fragile look of a little girl, but it was too late to change now.

Why was he dressed so impeccably? Was he going somewhere, or had he already been? From the corner of the window she watched him climb the steps; he was dressed in tailored black trousers and a white silk shirt opened at the collar to display a glimpse of the deeply tanned chest and a shadowy darkness of fine hair where the button fastened.

Just watching him brought tears to her eyes. He was so fine, so handsome. How could she ever ... ever ... ever get him out of her aching heart?

Without knocking, he walked inside. As he stood in the doorway the sunlight struck his handsome features; his green eyes glimmered at her.

Biting her lip, she stole a quick look at his face, then looked around the room while her heart settled.

'Hello, Molly.' He spoke softly. 'It's good to have you back among the living.' His eyes dwelt on her.

'I—I feel as though the whole thing was a nightmare.' She gazed at the still wrinkled doily beneath the lamp.

'How's your ankle?'

'Fine.'

'Have you been eating well?' His eyes wouldn't leave hers, even if she looked away.

'I guess,' she said in a toneless voice.

Christopher stared down at her, a pretense of shock on his face. 'You guess? You mean you don't know if you're eating or not?'

Hurt and bewildered, she met his eyes. How could he question her appetite at a time like this? Did he believe her to be so cold and calculating that she could think of food after her heart had been broken into a thousand pieces. With nothing left to hold of her shattered dreams, how could she sit down and eat?

'Eating has not been foremost in my mind, Christopher,' she said. 'For a fact, I've hardly given food a thought.'

'And what have you been thinking about?'

He walked over and sat down on the sofa near her chair.

She shook her head against the pillow.

Christopher's black eyebrows drew together above the bridge of his straight nose. 'Are you angry with me, Molly?' he asked.

Angry? No, I'm not angry with you.' She attempted a bleak smile. 'I can't blame you for doing what you must do, Christopher. And I can never be angry with you for doing it. I understand.'

'And what have I done, Molly?' he asked quietly. 'What is it you understand?'

At that moment Cora brought in the tea. 'Teatime. Teatime,' she said lightly. Then: 'Good morning, Chris.' She placed the tray on the table and poured tea into the cups.

'Hello, Cora. How are you?'

'I'm fine, but I'm not dressed yet, dear. It seems I can never get going until I've had my tea.' She lifted the cup to her lips.

'Are you going somewhere?' Molly asked, turning to her aunt.

'Yes,' Cora returned, surprised. 'Have you not told her, Chris?'

Christopher shook his head. 'Not yet.'

'Oh my!' Cora jumped up. 'Here, let me take my tea to my room. I can dress and drink at the same time.'

After she had left the room, Molly cast a quizzical look at him. This time it was he who refused to meet her eyes.

'Do you love me, Molly?' he asked, his voice deep and serious, his eyes resting on the cup in his hands.

'Yes,' she said without hesitation. 'You know I do.'

'Do you want to marry me?'

His unexpected question had taken her breath away; she was speechless for a moment. 'Yes,' she said faintly. 'You know I do.'

For a very brief moment he looked into her eyes. 'Very soon, I could become penniless. All I will have to my name is sixty pounds.'

She felt herself go weak. He was giving in to the LeDukes. She felt herself go taut as steel. She could not allow it. She would not allow it!

'Have I shocked you?' he asked softly. 'Well, don't be shocked. I am not going to cower before the LeDukes' demands.' He reached across and gripped her hand. 'I love you, Molly. You are more important to me than my land or any of my possessions. I know this, but still I cannot allow myself to meet their greedy demands, for if I did this, how bitter toward them would I be in the days to come for taking something I love away from me because I dared not to love Lydia.' His brilliant green eyes were deeply disturbed.

'Christopher, I don't understand.' She was regaining some of her strength. 'They will file suit against you. I know they will.'

He gave a short laugh. 'What is it you Americans say? You can't get blood out of a beet ... uh ... carrot ... or some bloody vegetable.'

'A turnip,' she whispered.

'At any rate, that is the predicament they will find themselves in. I have just returned from an overnight trip to England. My assets there have been transferred to my mother, and now, in a few minutes, I shall sell my land and home here.'

'Christopher! You can't! Don't you see, they won't stop. They'll get the money you've paid for the land. Don't you see?'

'You don't understand, my darling,' he announced. 'I am selling my land and home for sixty pounds. I doubt they will bother with a court battle for a mere sixty pounds.'

'Sixty pounds?' she echoed, her eyes wide. 'How can you?'

'Molly.' Suddenly he was in front of her, holding her hands tight in his own. 'When you find the right buyer, you can make the damnedest deals. I am selling my land to Cora. I have already sold her my cattle.'

'Aunt Cora? Molly's eyes filled with wonder. 'Aunt Cora?' She stared into his face, with its sun-darkened skin and determined lines drawn along the mouth.

'God in heaven, Molly. I love you. I fought it because I was told you came here to take advantage of a dear lady and her possessions. But you kept disturbing my thoughts at all hours of the day and night. If I was with my cattle, I found myself not paying heed to my chores but thinking of your sun-streaked hair, clean and shiny, with the scent of summer. Your eyes; your large blue eyes. God in heaven, no matter what I was doing I couldn't do anything but think of you. And all the while I thought you despised me. I couldn't believe that you loved me. It was just too good to be true.'

'I have loved you, Christopher, as long as, if not longer than, you have loved me.'

His thin tapered fingers curled over hers, the pressure increasing as he spoke. 'We shall have our chance at happiness, Molly. I promise you.'

She sat very still, accepting the fact that a very special kind of happiness was hers. A warm contented feeling flooded her.

He took her in his arms, and suddenly her breath was gone. He kissed her, and when their lips met, her soul filled with love and longing for him.

'I'm sorry I hurt you at the hospital, my darling.' He pressed his cheek against hers. 'I couldn't bear to hear you call out anoth—'

'Hush,' she interrupted in a whisper. 'I

211

should have waited to speak until I could say the complete sentence, but I didn't realize until I began that I couldn't. But that, like so many things, is past now, Christopher.'

The heartbeat throughout her body leaped with warmth and desire for him. She had never known this feeling before Christopher, and she would never know it without him. Her arms tightened around his neck.

'I love you, Christopher,' she murmured. 'I love you.'

'We will honeymoon right here on this island,' he said softly. 'We'll be together until you grow tired of me. We'll go sailing on the *Rainbow*, picnic on the beach.'

Molly pulled back and looked at him, her wide blue eyes searching his. 'The *Rainbow*?' she asked softly.

'Did you think I would leave her in the bay?' he teased gently. 'What kind of brute do you think I am, Molly Rayner?' With his fingertips he smoothed back the hair that had fallen across her forehead.

'Christopher.' She reached for him, shaking her head. His soothing masculine scents set her head spinning as his mouth swept down on hers. He kissed her quickly, then released her.

Standing, he gazed down at her with wide green eyes. 'Is Saturday too soon?'

'Saturday?'

'To be married. My parents will fly in from England, and Cora will be there. I know it won't be a large wedding, but under the circumstances I think that will be best.'

A pause. 'I don't know about Saturday,' Molly ventured with a slow deliberation. 'It will all depend on whether or not you finish my portrait. I don't think I could live in a house with a faceless picture hanging on my wall.'

He laughed softly. 'Well, my darling, if that's our only problem, we have none. That portrait was finished that very night after you left. I painted the remainder of the night.' Suddenly he glanced over his shoulder.

Cora Newcomb, dressed impeccably, stood in the doorway. 'Can you imagine a woman my age buying more land? Heavens! It just gives me something else to bequeath.'

Molly edged forward in the chair. 'Please hurry back,' she whispered.

Christopher stared at her a moment, winked, then moved to the doorway beside Cora. He smiled. 'We'll be back before you even realize we're gone.'

'I doubt that.' Molly smiled.

A moment later she watched the car turn in the drive and disappear over the rise. She leaned back against the pillow. Tropic sweetness filled the air, sliding through the open window on a breeze and mingling with the lingering scent of Christopher's after-shave. Molly Rayner sighed happily.

In the garden the little tui bird broke forth with his song. Closing her eyes, Molly listened to the clear bell-like notes.